THE OWNER'S TALE

Tales from the Longview: Episode 6

HOLLY LISLE

The Owner's Tale

Tales from the *Longview* #6

HOLLY LISLE

———————

Published by OneMoreWord Books

Tales from The Longview, Episode 6: The Owner's Tale

Cover Design: Holly Lisle

Cover Art: © Forgiss, 3000AD, from BigStockPhoto.com

Holly's Author Photo: © Holly Lisle

Copyright © 2018 by Holly Lisle

Content Editor: Matthew Turano at MattContentEdits.com

PUBLISHER'S NOTICE

This is a work of fiction. Seriously. Resemblances to real characters, real solar systems, real spaceships, and real faster-than-light travel are entirely coincidental. Names, characters, places, and tech are products of the author's imagination, and any brilliant guy who appears halfway through the story is not your cousin Bob, no matter how much he insists otherwise.

EPUB ISBN: 978-1-62456-061-3

KINDLE ISBN: 978-1-62456-062-0

For Matt

Chapter One

WERIX KEYR

N ow...

You know me as Werix Keyr, and by now, because you know what I am, you think you know me.

I am a monster — but that is **not** who I started out to be.

On this, the last day of my life, I want you to know how I became a monster. And why I did what I did.

And the truth is that, though I am a monster who has done terrible things, I did one wonderful thing as well.

For that one wonderful thing to live, to grow its wings, to become what settled space needs it to be, I have to die now. But I would not have you think ill of the dead.

Perhaps if I show you who I really am, you won't.

Chapter Two

CADENCE DRAKE

Twenty-Four Hours Earlier...

Cady came through the Bailey's Station origami point spot-welded to the front curve of a tiny transparent sphere, with the pain of being folded through space a fire along every nerve, and with the urge to vomit fighting whatever they'd shot her full of before they sealed her into the bait ball.

The words of the bastard who'd welded her into the ball echoed in her ears — "You'll get to see people die today. Your dear friend Fedara Contei, that criminal Wils Bailey, and every piece of breathing scum on or around that station. You'll see the end of Bailey's Irish. And Bailey's Point. You could have watched that monster lover of yours die, too — but Herog managed to get himself killed being stupid."

And he'd laughed at the shock on her face. And then injected something into her shoulder that hurt like hell.

"Don't want you to die before we can kill you," he said, and grinned. "That's to keep you from vomiting and drowning in your own puke when you go through the fold.

We want all you folks to be wide awake and kicking so your friends know they have to do what we tell them if they want us to save you."

"What do you want them to do?" she'd asked.

"Just hold still while we kill them," he told her. "You'll be our bait and our shields." And he'd smacked her on the ass and said, "Shame to waste you."

And then set the weapons systems behind her, turned on the air recycler, and sealed her into the capsule alone.

She found herself looking at a little boy spot-welded into a ball across from her. He was screaming and crying, fighting against his bonds. Dark skin like hers, dark eyes, thick black hair.

She caught his attention by making faces at him, then shook her head. He started watching her. Calmed down a little.

She mouthed the words, "You'll be all right." Smiled.

He looked disbelieving, and then she thought she read, "Where's Mommy?" in the words he mouthed to her.

"Mommy is safe," she said.

Which was not just a lie, but a damned lie, because odds were good that if his mother wasn't with him, she was in the same deep trouble Cady and the boy were in.

But the truth would not help the child survive what came next.

So Cady mimed sleeping and said, "Home to Mommy…" and "You're going home to Mommy," and hoped that would somehow turn out to be the truth in a happy sense rather than the other possibility, which was that they were all going to die horribly either during the point crossing or afterwards, and that either nothingness or whatever followed death would be all that remained of their future.

The bastard who'd bonded her to the inside of her

transparent cage had said she'd be going through a fold in it — and Cady had done that before, awake and alert. Two hundred ninety-seven times already.

Going through in this pathetic moleibond cage would make two hundred ninety-eight.

Had she been a commercial TFN pilot rather than an indie, she would have had one more sanctioned crossing in her career, after which she would have had the option to be grounded, or the option most of the big TFN pilots took, which was to walk into the infinite during their final crossing and see what waited on the other side.

She no longer believed that anything waited there. Her reality consisted of what she could prove… and nothing else.

But it didn't mean that she wouldn't see Badger again when she was folded through space…

Or Herog. If he was really dead, if the bastard who'd laughed about his death had been telling the truth, would she see Herog?

Their captors had gathered and were rolling the balls into little ground-to-space shuttles.

She allowed herself to drift into sleep. Was awakened when she was rolled back out of the shuttle onto what looked like a giant slingshot in the hold of a warship.

There was no gravity, so she was in space, and the hold didn't have gravity turned on — probably to facilitate the launching of these individual pods ahead of her.

So she was up against it now. Helpless, she faced the coming pain and darkness as Herog had taught her.

I am the only self I can prove, mine is the only reality I can prove. Everything that is coming is shadows and images. I matter, my choices matter, my actions matter, my life matters.

She was upside-down relative to the person in the ball

in front of her, who was facing away from her. She could see a line of transparent spheres ahead of her.

Each ball would be launched through the point, and she and the other hostages would be held in front of her friends in Bailey's as threats — that if they acted, she and the others would be killed.

But if they did not act, they would still be killed.

She tried to figure out how she could warn them, and then the ball made a half rotation forward and stopped. They'd started firing.

There was no sound. There was nothing but the silence of deep space. She could shout and hear her own voice, but there was no atmosphere outside of the balls, so the sound did not carry.

She closed her eyes. Her cage rolled forward. *Count*, she thought, and counted, "One-one-thousand, two-one-thousand, three-one-thousand, four-one-thousand" and rolled forward again.

A four-second launch clock was fairly loose.

But she realized that the threat had to have teeth, and that something that could kill the hostage had to be going through, too.

If she were shooting hostages into a location, she'd put something behind the hostage to make sure no one got any funny ideas about a rescue...

Two-second launch clock. And the threats going through in between. That was more likely what was going on, and that was tight.

She'd learned a lot about fighting in space from Herog.

Closed her eyes. If she saw him when she pushed through the fold, when she fell into the infinite and linked to the phantasms of her mind — or the truth of the Infinite — did that mean he was truly dead?

And she remembered Herog asking her the question

that had changed everything for her. "If this were the only reality, what would you do differently?"

She also remembered her answer. "I'd fight harder. I'd never quit."

This is the only reality I can prove, she told herself again. *This is the only reality I know I can reach. So I must act on the theory that my life matters, my actions matter, and when I die, I die completely and forever.*

I want to live. So I will do everything I can to live.

The balls before her rolled forward. Forward. Forward.

And then she was next...

And launched...

The Infinite Other crushed her into an infinite number of separate parts, and Badger was in there calling to her, and Herog was standing there staring at her in a thousand guises, and in some of them he begged her to come join him.

But the Herog she knew, the one who was true to everything that was Herog, held on inside her mind, and that Herog said, "It's a reflection of reality. It is not reality. Live, Cady."

"Live, Cady," she whispered, hanging on through the shattering, the scattering, the breaking apart of everything she was into everything she might ever have been or might ever be, through the twisting, wrenching, tearing pain, through the lure of death which was the end of all pain...

"Live... Cady."

Through her two hundred ninety-eighth passage through madness.

She came out the other end whispering, "Live, Cady. Live."

Chapter Three

My first name was K-Eighty-Four.

By definition, I was born a monster.

On the little moon of Beckenridge, where the Beckenridge Colony of Living Saints exists to this day, a Breeder gave birth to me and put me into the *bernekaste* with other infants and small children, to be fed and cleaned and trained by a stream of older children until I reached puberty.

Cultures define monstrosity differently, and not all definitions are true.

Some actions are genuinely evil, and some monsters define their evil as goodness. And to the extent that the world into which I was born was monstrous in its own right, the fact that the Saints would have defined me as a monster speaks more to their villainy than to mine.

But in the end, your own choices are what make you a monster.

By choice, I became a monster by any civilized definition.

But first, the beginning. I was born into the Sacred

Death of the Living Saints, where breeding is duty, where no desires are permitted, where life is proof of one's evil, and death is the gate to reward.

From the time I was old enough to know I drew breath, to understand language, to walk and run, I was filled with desire. I was attracted to both the girls in the *bernekaste* and the boys. And on the inside, I desired them as both a female and a male.

The first thing you learn in the *bernekaste* is that anything that makes you different gets you punished.

So the first thing I learned was to do a very good impression of being a normal child. I was better looking than most of the children, and any sort of attractiveness is a sin in a world where something that causes desire is a sin. So I worked to make myself plain, ungainly, awkward.

But I was also intelligent. Another sin — a much bigger one — because intelligence introduces the question "Why?" to the mind, and sows the seeds of doubt against authority.

Intelligence is something bright children reveal by accident, but that a very intelligent child can figure out how to hide. I learned to be observant, to be obedient, to be dull and slow in my responses, to hold my tongue, to bow my head, to keep my thoughts to myself. To stutter and fumble for words, to look blankly at those in authority who questioned me about my actions.

Being stupid is not a sin — it is among the Saints a sign of Divinely imposed obedience. The stupid do not question. They simply accept.

As I grew older, I allowed myself no friends.

To the Saints, friendship is a sin — it creates a value that stands between the living and the Path to Death. One might value a friend enough to want to save that friend from death, and if death is the reward for the punishment of life, then anything that impedes the downward slide to the grave is evil.

Saints classify male children on their Day of Readiness as Second Saints, Monk, or Slave. Their two classifications for girls are Breeder and Cull.

Second Saints, subservient only to the Saint himself, do no physical work. They live in fine stone houses and spend a small portion of their day in prayer, and a large portion of their day in eating, drinking, and breeding, or practicing their breeding skills on those who cannot conceive, whether because of age or because of gender. This is, they insist, not because they are filled with desire, but because they are obedient to duty. It is the duty of the Saints to be ever ready to breed more Saints, and this requires much practice.

Second Saints also do the classification of each child brought before them.

Monks, neutered on their Classification Day and treated with occasional kindness, carry out the higher-level tasks of running the colony — tending to the machines and the histories and the recording of the birthrights and lineages of the Breeders and their offspring.

Slaves, neutered and despised, do the dirty work. And there is immense dirty work in a place like Beckenridge Colony. Not just the cleaning, the clearing, the building, the planting, the harvesting, the tending of the beasts.

There is also the taking of children to the Saints for whatever purposes the Saints might require, including but not limited to their final classification.

Breeders and Culls reach their Day of Classification when they are Marked by Sin. Girls marked as Breeders stay to tend children until they are successfully bred. Once they catch, they are placed in corrals where they stay until they have given birth. Once they are delivered of their

Proof of Sin, they may be marked Shamed with Life, and kept for further breeding. If the creature they give birth to is damaged in any way, however, they are proved free of sin, and are Honored with Death.

Culls…

Well, on their Day of Classification, Culls are Honored with Death.

Not only are they released to The End of Suffering, but they become… useful.

Culls Honored with Death are part of the other duties of the slaves. The Saints kill these girl children in some sort of ritual, and once they're dead, the slaves make their bodies into fertilizer, bonemeal, leather for wallets, food for pigs…

Friendless and to all appearances clumsy, awkward, and stupid, I could have survived among the Saints except for the final accident of my birth.

Because while the first thing I learned was to pretend to be normal, the second thing I learned is that no matter what anyone says about the holiness of Classification, or about Great Holy's Demand and the sacred duty of every child to submit, there is no good ending for you if you're born female.

Breeder.

Or Cull.

All this I saw. All this I watched sidelong, quietly, saying nothing, thinking always. I demonstrated my slow wit, my bovine complacency with my lot. I kept my head down and made myself look as plain as I could.

But as I neared puberty, I could see the boys in the *bernekaste* looking at me more than they looked at the other girls. They were noting the change of my shape, responding as unneutered males do.

Male children are allowed to be beautiful because they

may be chosen to be Saints. The Saints want plain women, though, because they will not be objects of desire. They will simply be objects of convenience for the making of new Saints.

I could not make myself plain enough, and because of this, I could see my death approaching.

Those who die soonest serve best. So teach the Saints.

While I could not know the date of my death, I had no doubt that when I was brought before the Saints for classification, I would be a Cull.

One of the throats cut, one of the bodies drained of blood, just another thing for the slaves to run through the grinder after everything else had been stripped from me.

But when we labored in the fields with the Slaves, tending and picking crops, I could also see each month the supply ship that dropped to the landing pad on the far side of the colony. The men who offloaded the supplies. No one from the colony was permitted to approach these men. They were unclean, damaged — *bojaats*.

I thought that if I could just offer something they might want, I might survive.

By the time I had conceived my escape plan, I was, by my best guess, eleven standard years old. Perhaps twelve. I was tying strips around my chest under my shirt to hide my budding breasts. Was dreading the Mark of Sin which would send me before the Saint, and I was desperate to figure a way that I might hide it when it came so that I might survive a little longer.

I knew only that I did not want to die. Not in that place. Not for those people.

So I found a place where I might mark time, and I marked each day from the time the supply ship left until it returned. And each month, I watched and waited for an opportunity.

Finally, two days by my hidden count before the supply ship was due to come again, I crept out at night, slipping quietly behind the girl who was senior in the *bernekaste*, who had been classified as a Breeder, but who was not yet bred, and who had been called to be obedient to the Saints. Once she was out of sight, I crept through the darkness, staying ever in shadow, and found my way to the landing pad. There I dug a hole for myself in which I could hide, and when I was in it, stripped naked, folded my clothes over my head, and pulled dried leaves and a little dirt into the hole on top of them.

And then I waited.

I ate nothing.

I drank my own piss, gathered as best I could from one cupped hand. I did not allow myself to shit. I had to be as presentable as I could make myself when the *bojaats* came, because I was going to offer myself to them as a Breeder if they would just take me with them. I hoped that they would see me as such, instead of as a Cull.

While I hid, I could hear searchers looking for me. Could hear their shouts, their feet thudding, their calling of my number. Screaming, "K-Eighty-Four!"

I held still whenever they neared, breathing shallowly, wedged with my back against the hole, with my eyes closed tight, praying to anything that might save me that they would not accidentally trip into my hole.

And late the second day, when the partial dark of the folded clothes and leaves over my head was dimming to the true dark of night, I heard the arrival of the supply ship.

I waited until I heard the ramp open, until I heard the voices of the men who brought things I could neither identify or imagine for the use of the Saints, and then I dressed and climbed out of the hole.

I wiped my hands as clean as I could with the leaves,

untied the bindings from around my breasts, scrubbed my face as best I could with my spit and one of the balled-up bindings, ran my fingers through my hair. I wanted to make myself look as good as I could.

And I walked up to the first man I reached, and even though he was doing work like a Monk, said, "If you will take me with you, I will be your personal Breeder."

He stared at me, yelled back to the ship, then made a gesture and said a string of words I did not understand.

I wondered if he was mad or damaged in some way. Another man, differently dressed and looking more important, more like a Saint and less like a Monk, came out of the ship, said something to the man who'd called him with the same meaningless sounds. Then he studied me, and said, "You should not be here."

"I will be a Cull," I said. "I do not want to be a Cull, so if you will take me with you, I will be your personal Breeder."

I saw his eyes widen, then narrow. "Anyone know you're here?"

"The Saints know I'm gone. They have looked for me for two days, but have not yet found me."

"Get into the ship," he said. "You can come with us. What's a Cull?"

When I told him, he first laughed, then realized I was truthful. He said, "That's wrong. Evil. I won't be a part of that. This is the last delivery I'll take to a Saints' colony."

And it was. Durbin Anrish was a better man than the Saints.

Not so good, however, that he refused my offer. I became — for six years — his personal Breeder, though I did not catch while he bred me.

Chapter Four

WHEN I WAS TADRA AMU

Durbin refused to call me K-Eighty-Four. He said I could have any name I wanted, and he'd make it legal. And I thought of the important names among the Living Saints. I recalled the god-name of the most important man in the colony and said, "Could my name be A-One?"

He burst out laughing. Said, "By all the… No, that's not a name. Tell you what. In the language of my people, the words for 'volunteered love' are *tadra amu*. How would that do as a name for now? You can change it when you come up with something better, but in the meantime, it'll give me something to call you, and something to register for you when we buy you an identity."

"Tadra Amu." I tried it on for size. Shrugged. Back then, I didn't see what was wrong with my own name.

What can I say? I was young, which is a disability that fortunately passes.

But I was also curious. "Why do you have to buy me an identity?"

He said, "They don't teach you much in that colony, do they?"

I shrugged.

He sighed. "If you're on my ship and you don't have a legal Gen-ID, or some other confirmed, testable identification, the first time we have to go through a secure checkpoint it's going to look like I kidnapped you. There are places where we can buy you a backstory, tag it to your genetic code, put you on the roster as paid crew, and you can work for me. If we have a relationship on the side, that's our business."

The relationship on the side, I'll note, was our main business. But he did have me help the crew, he did pay me, and when I saw a crew member drawing in his off-time, and showed an interest in learning how to do that, Durbin showed me how to sign up for onboard art training. I bought a couple of Senso art courses and from them learned basics and some advanced techniques.

And when I was too old to be of interest to Durbin anymore, he helped me apply to various art schools. On the strength of my work, I was accepted by the Oldcity University of Fine Arts at Meileone on Cantata on partial scholarship.

When he dropped me off on Cantata, he went his way and never looked back.

So I had no one in settled space who cared about me when I walked into the university. No parents, no siblings, no friends. I was the perfect target. And I was pretty — something that Durbin had emphasized was both an important and a good quality in a woman who wasn't trapped in a Living Saints colony.

A lot of young men and a few women in my classes and in the dormitory expressed attraction to me, but being nineteen — at least according to my purchased ident — and having just gotten out of a six-year relationship, I was not interested in romance.

I was interested in discovering who I might become.

In my first six months at the university, I learned everything I could about art, digging deep into history, techniques, mediums, and philosophies. I fell in love with Alien Hyperrealism, and started producing my first body of work.

In the little free time I allowed myself, I explored the science behind genderflipping. It appealed to me — on Cantata, if I could just make enough money, I could be either male or female at any given time, and I would finally be able to make the outside of me match the inside.

But at the time it was far too expensive for me to even consider, so I resigned myself to being just a part of who I was until I could become a rich, famous artist.

Take a moment to laugh with me here. Those who pursue the arts hoping to become rich and famous are like all the grains of sand in a desert. Those who do it? They're the grains that get picked up in a sandstorm and dropped into an upturned thimble in the middle of the desert's only oasis.

But again... Youth and innocence. I thought if I did the work, I would become renowned throughout settled space.

So when, at a showing of student art, I met a wealthy, important man who loved my work and raved about my brilliance and genius, I thought my moment had come already. He told me he was a Councillor in Oldcity, and the president of a group of dedicated art collectors called the Universal Society of Antiquarian Gothicans.

His name was Danniz Oe, and he was intelligent, well-versed in art, funny, charming, good-looking... and rich enough to be the sole patron for an artist like me. I would, he told me, be the best investment he'd ever made.

We had a few drinks to celebrate.

And then went to my little apartment together.

And things got...

Blurry.

I woke up in a dark room, alone. Not my room. Some-place I'd never seen before.

I was hungry. No. I was ravenous. I was lost, I was confused, I couldn't remember where I was or how I'd come to be there.

But I could smell food. The best food I'd ever smelled in my whole life.

I followed the smell, not thinking this was strange behavior for me. I stayed in the shadows, in the dark places, because light bothered my eyes. I walked up behind the magnificent smell of food that had called me to it, grabbed the container — vaguely recognizing it as human but incapable of stopping myself — and ripped it open with teeth that had reshaped themselves into daggers.

I drank.

Deeply and long, with the perfect taste of blood flowing along my tongue, filling me with heat and strength and contentment.

And in the instant after I recognized that contentment, sanity returned.

I looked at the dead woman I was holding up with one hand — and realized that suddenly I was strong enough to do that. She was chubby. Older. Wore servant's clothing. I knew that I had killed her. I knew that I'd drunk her blood. I dropped her.

Then, because I was still hungry, I got down on my

hands and knees and licked the spilled blood around her off the inlaid marble floor. I felt repugnance at what I was doing. I felt the human I had once been still inside me, screaming at my actions.

But the perfect nectar that was her blood called to me, and I did not stop until I'd licked up every spilled drop.

Chapter Five

23 HOURS EARLIER...

Cady couldn't believe what she'd witnessed.

The battle should have been insanely uneven. The combined forces of the Pact Worlds Alliance and the two militaries with which it had allied should have been able to destroy the tiny, cobbled-together fleet that protected Bailey's Irish Space Station and Bailey's Point in mere seconds.

Cady's bait ball had been pulled over toward the station the instant it pushed through the origami point.

From her vantage point, she could see more balls pushing through, and two seconds behind each one, a pirate ship.

She watched the complex maneuvering of bait balls, getting a feel for the curving wall they would have built had they been left in place, seeing the kind of human shield they would have made for the pirate vessels coming in behind.

She knew this wasn't a pirate attack. She knew this was a front, a pretense. That the Pact World Alliance had declared war on the station using the pirates. Had the

PWA just come through the point on their own, they could have destroyed the station in seconds.

Why hadn't they?

Hanging soundless in space, pinned in a position where she had to look at what was happening, knowing that behind and beneath her, rescuers were disarming the weapons inside the bait ball that would have killed front-on rescuers and her, watching more people like her being pushed through to provide cover for pirates, watching the pirates being destroyed with the same efficiency that the bait balls were being rescued, she had nothing she could do but think.

So she thought.

The Pact Worlds Alliance was determined to make a show of its might. To make sure everyone in settled space knew the horrors that would befall any world that dared to offer sanctuary to someone the PWA had declared an enemy. Who dared to stand against it.

By sending pirates to do the actual destruction, it was proving that even pirates obeyed it. Would serve its will.

This massive pirate army that was being slaughtered one ship at a time, this massive collection of hostages being rescued one bait ball at a time, was not here to threaten Bailey's Irish Space Station, or Bailey's Point.

Cady had no doubt that the pirates would have been set loose in the station. Would have raped and pillaged, would have murdered and taken slaves.

But this wasn't about the people in the station. And it wasn't even about Bailey's Point.

The PWA certainly had other hidden agents in place on the station like those who had kidnapped her — people who were creating proof of what was happening to Bailey's Point. The PWA would be recording everything so once Bailey's was destroyed, the rest of settled space could see what happened to dissenters.

After Bailey's Point dared to defy the Pact Worlds Alliance and offer sanctuary to the *Longview*, the PWA would consider the massacre of every man, woman, and child in the system a prudent demonstration of its power.

So it was sending it its pirate allies, and she suspected it planned to come in after them and finish off anything the pirates hadn't destroyed, then declare itself the One Government of Settled Space — just as, following mass slaughter of every citizen in Free Novatia nearly a hundred years earlier, the United Bloc had declared itself the One Government of Old Earth.

Cady thought Bailey's Point was intended to be the PWA demonstrating that it could go anywhere, do anything, destroy anyone who stood against it.

But...

Whatever the PWA had planned was going badly wrong. So far.

Suddenly, her perspective shifted as she was turned around and dragged toward the station. Toward the far end and then inside.

Reflected from behind her in the shiny surface of the bait ball, she saw the flash of an explosion.

Thought "that could have been me."

She closed her eyes and yearned for Herog.

Chapter Six

WHEN I WAS SUCCESSFUL TRANSMISSIBLE
NANOVIRUS PROTOTYPE 01

Tadra Amu was declared dead. One dismembered finger, her spilled blood, signs of violent struggle in her on-campus apartment, her abandoned paintings and her abandoned scholarship were held as proof of her death. There was no one to notify. So no one was notified, and after cursory investigation, the matter was dropped.

Me?

I went from being an art student to being Danniz Oe's *Successful Transmissible Nanovirus Prototype 01*. I was the first human Oe drank dry who didn't die.

Instead of dying, I acquired the nanovirus through bite transmission, survived, and became a Legend like Oe. The first proof of concept that Oe's vision of a universe in which immortal gods could own all of humanity as their slaves was given real shape and form, and could make their own slaves through both mind control — over those lesser creatures, mere humans — and over the powerful, dangerous creatures they created by transmission. I was the first powerful slave of the first powerful lineage. I was the first proof that the vampire mythos both Danniz Oe and his friend and original funding partner Gainer Holloway wanted to turn into reality could could come true.

Gainer Holloway immediately tripled his investment, injected himself with Oe's adaptation of the Legend nanovirus, and became, like Oe, a top-level immortal.

Oe and Holloway called me StranP01, pronounced Stran-poy.

Danniz Oe was living his dream. Through me and those people he fed to me, once every two weeks during the first two years of experimentation he tested adaptations of the nanovirus — improving its transmissibility; decreasing the need for frequent feeding but increasing the obligatory feeding mechanism (where when you got hungry enough you lost your mind and any ethics you had and attacked and slaughtered the first human who crossed your path); increasing the "creator vampire" control over the creatures made from his bite. I lived through those years chained to a wall in the basement of his mansion, and every upgrade or minor adaptation he did on the nanovirus he tested first on me. He then starved me until I lost my mind, and fed me new innocents to see how they turned out.

Oe focused on "bite lineage" as the most important feature of the body mod he was building. This gave me command over the monsters my bite had created, but because he commanded me, gave him power over them that overrode any commands I might give. By the third year of his testing, he had turned me into a creature incapable of taking any action against him, and through me, he had a growing band of nearly indestructible immortals absolutely obedient to his every utterance.

He was living his dream… but his dream was my worst nightmare.

My thoughts were my own. I knew who I was, I knew

who I'd been, I remembered what I'd wanted. What I still wanted — to create, to live a good life, to find independence and happiness.

But my actions belonged to Danniz Oe. He sent me out to do things I found horrific, and while my mind rebelled, my body obeyed.

When I'd fed, when I was alone, everything that had always mattered to me still mattered to me, but when I was hungry, the obligate feeding response Oe had built into the mod took over, and I grabbed a human, brought that person to one of Oe's stations, drank the blood, left my victim where I'd found it... and roughly ninety percent of the time, my victim would be so quickly infected by the nanoviral mod that it would live rather than die, would curl up in the room where I'd left it, where it would have a horrible three days of transformation, after which it would crawl out hungry, would attack and drink dry some innocent in the vicinity, and would become a monster like me.

Obedient to me, but *more* obedient to my master. My power grew with every new Legend I created, but because he made more first-level slaves like me with whom he built more lineages for himself, his power grew exponentially faster.

His friend Holloway was busy building his own lineage of obedient slaves.

It was the ultimate pyramid scheme, in which those at the top became gods.

Occasionally Danniz or Holloway would acquire control of another planet by bringing in someone already rich and important person on that world to become a USAG member. For an exorbitant up-front fee, they would make that owner a legend beneath them. Then they would collect USAG dues from that world's new Secret Dark God.

The two of them were franchising immortality and godhood, and there were a lot of buyers.

After their biggest breakthrough with me as their test subject, three more years passed, during which Oe and Holloway made a massive amount of money selling the real version of an ancient Old Earth mythology in which undead blood drinkers were the secret masters of a world.

Three years, during which the Legend population on Cantata grew slowly and carefully, sold one bite at a time to the highest bidders, hidden from discovery by the people in high places who had paid well to become part of it...

During which the richest, the most famous, and the most powerful people on Cantata joined the immortals at the TOP level, just beneath Oe and Holloway, to change the Universal Society of Antiquarian Gothicans — USAG - from a group of fantasy vampire recreators into the masters of that terrifying fantasy made real.

During which, under the guise of being a quaint little group of ancient literature buffs, these god-pretenders set up their organization to further the following goals, written right into their well-hidden bylaws:

- To turn all civilized worlds and settlements in Settled Space into primitive societies driven by superstition and ignorance
- To place USAG members in charge of every world and colony in Settled Space as the Immortal Gods of these societies
- To require USAG members to rule their worlds with fear, slaughter, and torture — the values of the Vampire Mythos — claiming everything of value for themselves and being worshipped eternally by their hapless human slaves

But here's the thing…

Oe was brilliant at modifying the nanovirus he'd acquired from elsewhere. He had astonishing skills in viral engineering.

He was, however, surprisingly bad at simple arithmetic.

I wasn't. At the point where he and Holloway had stopped adapting the virus, I'd proven myself useful in other ways. I was very good at math. As the first slave, I was utterly trustworthy because I could not disobey him — and because I'd demonstrated that I was capable recognizing opportunities for profit, he'd put me in charge of handling all of his money from all of its sources.

At this point, when I could see the whole picture, I identified what he was doing as a pyramid scheme, and I found the horrific flaw in his business model.

If you create immortals who create immortals and the immortals not only eliminate one source of food ninety-eight out of every hundred times they feed directly from a living human — because not everyone they fed from died — but also, ninety out of a hundred times create a new immortal who also needs to feed, sooner rather than later you're going to wipe out your food source.

Legends in the "published" version of his nanovirus were only driven to obligate feeding about once a month — or when they were injured and lost a lot of blood. And most kept a supply of humans on hand from whom they simply drew blood that they drank in events they called *tastings*, as if they were wine connoisseurs. So initially the problem grew slowly.

But very few of people who bought in at the "one vampire beneath Oe or Holloway" level limited themselves to tastings. Quite a few wanted slaves like me who would make them more powerful. Which in turn made Oe and

Holloway more powerful, so both of those idiots encouraged these bits of expansion.

And none of Oe's top-level feeders took any responsibility for regulating the feeding of the creatures they created, because every single new vampire in their downline gave them more personal power.

While in the early years, the expanding Legend population grew slowly, it still grew exponentially.

I kept this bit of math to myself. I needed to stay on Oe's good side, to remain his loyal, trusted slave StranP01.

Why?

Because along with showing me that he was a fool endangering the human species — something he would not believe even if I showed him the math — I'd also discovered that my work for him had a benefit that might eventually give me my freedom.

Chapter Seven

To serve Oe, I had to work in the world, and StranP01 was not a recognized entity.

So I obtained his permission to acquire a secure identity for myself. The only way to do this was illegal, of course — but through one interesting contact I'd made during the illegal work I was doing for Oe already, I tracked down a genius rumored to be flawless at creating bulletproof recreations with brilliant backstories. This genius had created his own identity and had become impossible to find except through recommendation. His name was Storm Rat. Through him, I became Fedara Contei.

Seven years from my conversion — with my proven skill at math and my flawless identity in place, and with my loyalty as Danniz Oe's absolute slave proven repeatedly — I was put in charge without oversight of handling Oe's finances and the finances of USAG. My mission, stated by my master in no uncertain terms, was to make him "god rich." He was immortal, he'd already made himself "god powerful," and he intended to live forever in the style to which he wanted to become accustomed.

The dues coming into USAG from his subservient Legends had to be invested, managed, made to grow.

To give me the best trainers, Oe brought in captured experts from a number of fields who taught me everything they knew about investing, financing, money laundering, extortion, and a number of other fascinating, useful skills, both legal and criminal. Once I'd learned everything they could teach me — and I forced them to teach me everything they knew simply by smiling at them and willing them to obey — Oe took them off to play with, then disposed of them invisibly.

He considered murdering anyone who'd had contact with me, and who might guess what I was doing, a reasonable precaution.

I used what I was taught, and began adding to his wealth. He knew he owned me body and soul. He knew I could do him no harm. And every single day, he could see me multiplying his wealth. He knew I was making him rich. "God rich."

And I did him no harm. Over the next seven years, he saw himself become one of the richest men in settled space.

However, because I had been tasked with making his wealth eternal, and because I could see that he made horrible investments when spending his money himself, I quickly came to understand that as his obedient slave, I had to do something to protect him from himself. So I diverted a significant portion of his income invisibly into a number of cautious investment accounts where the money just rolled over and grew at a healthy but safe interest rate. Oe was listed as the owner of these accounts, and since he had a lock on immortality, there should have been no need for a second account holder.

The accounts I chose, however, because they were legitimate, required both a primary and a secondary contact and a designated inheritor. I was the primary contact, given *carte blanche* by Oe to act as his right hand in all matters financial. In keeping him away from this section of his money, I was protecting Oe from himself and fulfilling my mandate to keep him permanently rich.

But I understand both the appearance and the fact of "conflict of interest" and as his financial manager, I knew that naming myself his backup inheritor would, by creating a conflict of interest, potentially harm him. So I invented a nonexistent creature as the second contact and backup inheritor.

Weyrix Keyr.

I was doing my owner no harm. I was, instead, benefitting him greatly. His wealth from these safe, hidden accounts was growing far better than the accounts he knew about, because they sat untouched, earning compound interest. He was not buying moons and colonies and doing ridiculous terraforming projects with them to create "perfect vampire havens," as he was with the money he could reach. He was getting "god rich," which meant that I was doing exactly what he'd told me to do.

In both the letter and the spirit of the constraints that bound me, I was obedient.

I invested him heavily in some of the most respectable businesses in settled space. Ancient art. Medical research. Slowship renovation and flipping. Settlement franchises. And I had one slowship refurbished into a Death Circus ship. It seemed a ridiculous waste of space. Slowships are massive, and Death Circuses make profits by quickly reselling their convicted criminals to people who have use for such creatures — as slaves, as gladiators, or for other less savory purposes.

I, however, was not terribly interested in reselling. I set up my ship with the requirement that all prisoners purchased by my franchise be stored permanently in special hibernation Medixes as long-term investments. They could only be sold when bidding on them reached one hundred thousand rucets. I stated that it was a requirement of the owner.

Oe, of course, had made no such requirement since he didn't even know he owned a Death Circus. And I had no logical reason for demanding that the main I hired as the Criminal Manager for the Death Circus do this. The steady selling of low-priced to mid-range Class A prisoners is how a Death Circus makes most of its profit, and my ridiculously high price meant that only a very few criminals would ever be sold.

I could not have explained to anyone why I took the actions with that Death Circus that I took. Not even to myself.

Looking back at myself as I was then, I recognize now that I was not alone inside myself.

Deep down, the part of me that had once been K-Eighty-Four still hid naked in a hole with leaves over her head — quiet, watchful, waiting. Operating her plans out of my sight. Knowing that at some point an opportunity for freedom might come, and that if it came, she wanted to be ready.

Down in the dark, she kept herself to herself, once again ready to move if that single chance to escape ever came.

Chapter Eight

ON HEROG'S FOURTH DAY IN THE CITY OF FURIES...

Herog sat at the round table, studying three citizens who made up the rest of the City of Furies' brand new defense council.

The council didn't have a name, didn't have a special office in a government building, didn't have flunkies or conveniences. No one except him was being paid to be there. The three volunteers had skills, knowledge, and a history of not dying when dying would have been the easy thing.

Ex-slaves like him, every one of them.

They'd been meeting every day for three days after their regular jobs. He'd spent every hour after his paid job — which was surveying the city's existing technology — trying to understand how the damned place hadn't already been discovered and wiped off the face of its planet.

It had walls, and no one could go outside the walls. Or come in through them. But walls had not been a viable defense since just past the dawn of civilization on Old Earth.

The woman on the committee, Derna, said, "We've

received confirmation that Bailey's Point now has access to all the warships and primary support ships from three fleets, and if they can find people to operate them, will own outright the biggest and most powerful military force in settled space. And the owner of the Longview wants Bailey's Point to become humanity's seat of power. He wants the Bailey's citizens to wipe out slavery and become the center of a spreading wave of individual rights and freedom." Derna's day job was fuel optimization research. Her personal history before she woke up in the City of Furies was something she did not talk about. "The owner of the *Longview*, who is the primary investor in most of the projects underway in this city, wants Bailey's Point to go on the offensive, to use all that power to start requiring other worlds to adopt the standards by which Bailey's Point operates."

Herog said, "I know. He was vehement about that. Like us, he was a slave. He would not go into his history with me, but there's a lot of rage in him even now."

"Taking the offensive seems logical," Meklen said. He did infrastructure design and had developed the streets, over-roads, and flight paths for the air cars. "And back when I was a slave, I would have given anything to see a military come in, wipe out all the slave owners, free us, and take us someplace safe. But something about this just doesn't sit right with me."

Derna and Liam, the almost-always-silent fourth member, nodded.

Derna said, "I'm all in favor of the eradication of slave owners. But I don't like the idea of it being done by a government. The slave hunters were heroes to me, but so were slaves like you. You — Herog. You got yourself free, you used everything they'd done to hurt you to make your-self stronger, and when you escaped you brought that down on them. The *first* time I got free, you and your people actually came through and pulled me out of…" she faltered. "Of where I was."

Herog looked at Derna and raised an eyebrow. In the years since he'd escaped, he and his allies had freed uncounted thousands of slaves, and he would not have recognized her. But he nodded. It made sense to him that some of the people he'd rescued would have ended up in the City of Furies.

He said, "I understand where Mado Keyr is coming from, but he's wrong. Dead wrong. He has a vision of a universe in which no one is ever a slave, but that vision includes the control of every single human being in order to prevent slavery from ever being able to arise again. It mandates the creation of an oppressive central government that forces its will on every human being alive. And the fact that he means well *means nothing.* He is working to create the system he hates, and he thinks that because he had good intentions, it will turn out differently than it has in every other place where people relinquished their power to a government and told the government to protect them. Giving any government that kind of power is the path to Hell."

"So… How do we keep this place safe? How do we protect our citizens, our creations, our philosophy?"

Herog stood up and started pacing. "How do you currently deal with people who come in here, who are spies or enemy agents, who attempt sabotage?"

He watched them look at each other, expressions of bewilderment on their faces. Derna said, "To the best of my knowledge, no such person has ever gotten into the city. There has never been an attempt at sabotage made — much less a successful one."

He stopped pacing. All three of them were nodding agreement.

"How then do you deal with other problems? With criminals, with homicides, with kidnappings or rapes or abuse?"

The puzzled expressions on their faces sent a little chill down his spine.

Derna said, "I... I don't know. I don't think there's ever been anything like that here."

The others nodded.

"How do you go about finding a missing child, then?"

And they all stared at each other. "I haven't even seen a child since I arrived here," Derna whispered.

"How about funerals of important people?"

"I supposed there have been," Liam, the fourth member of their panel, who was an engineer, looked at the other three. "If we checked for obituaries." He shrugged, "In the seventeen years I've lived here, I haven't heard of any deaths. But I haven't been looking for them."

Derna looked startled. "Since I came here, I haven't known a single person who has died."

Mecklen looked thoughtful. "Neither have I... But I never really thought about it. Everyone *I* know is young and healthy."

Herog said, "No crime, no abuse, no children, no old age, no death. You know what that means?"

They looked at him, shaking their heads.

"I do," he said. "I think Keyr already has his solution. He just doesn't realize it yet."

Chapter Nine

WHEN I WAS FEDARA CONTEI

Sometimes you know an individual is going to change your life the minute you meet him. Or this time, for me, *her*.

I met Cadence Drake on assignment from Oe. She had tripped over USAG, and was dangerously curious about it, and getting close to finding the truth.

But she was working for someone else, and Oe had been unable to discover who'd hired her.

So I was to contact her, enthrall her, and bring her to Oe... and then he was going to release her so I could go with her. She was to rescue me, take me with her back to whomever had hired her. I would go with her, kill her employer, and then kill her.

My orders were simple and clear, and up to a point, I obeyed the letter of them. The spirit of them? Well...

I discovered that Cady and her friend Badger had done complex worm searches that ran through the dark ping. Monitoring traffic on the dark ping had been what tipped off Danniz Oe.

But I also found out that Cady and Badger had uncovered Oe's franchise — the names of USAG's members, who were all first-level Oe slaves like me, but who had bought in to USAG as investment members, had bought their bite, and who were all rich. To Cady and Badger, it had become clear that the organization was more than rich Old-Earth pseudohistory buffs who liked to play dress-up while pretending to be dark-god immortals.

So Oe pulled me away from working on his finances, and took me to Galatia Fairing to gain control over Cadence Drake without converting her to one of us. I had to kill her when my mission was done, and Oe wanted the process to be as clean and efficient as possible.

I did not expect the impact she had on me the first time I met her.

I'll be blunt. *I wanted her.* She was intelligent, independent, brusque, funny, strange. So I did the sort of thing Oe would not have approved of... but had failed to forbid. Since it didn't pose any threat of harm to him, and since it might even prove helpful...

I did some personal research on her, on my own rucet and using and misusing the resources to which I had access on Galatia Fairing.

It turned out that Cady had the highest captain's exam scores I'd ever seen in someone I'd met. Better yet, her psych profiles marked her as brilliant, prone to ethics-driven disobedience and unsanctioned, independent action. Every report confirmed that she was poorly socialized and best kept away from any job that conferred real power. That she was captain of her own scrubby little ship and working independently, finding expensive things (and sometimes people) who had gone missing for high-paying clients. The life she had chosen made her a non-threat to people in charge of worlds, who would otherwise have been terrified of her.

I saw no indication in her history that she'd ever been attracted to women, and not much indication that she was attracted to men. Her relationship with Badger had started in their early childhoods, and while cautious digging suggested that they had been lovers on a few occasions, Badger had left a trail of broken hearts, both male and female, behind him wherever he went.

She...?

Had mostly been his friend, occasionally his sexual partner. From everything I could discover, she'd had a horrible childhood and brutal exit from Cantata back when she had been Tanasha Elenday. She was the estranged daughter of Lashanda Elenday, who was one of Oldcity's big movers and shakers, and one of Oe's top-level USAG members on Cantata.

Unlike her friend Badger, who'd had multiple serious romances before falling in love with her, Cady had never had a committed romantic love interest.

For me, that would have made her a difficult conquest, had I not been what I am.

Meanwhile, I, with my own awful history, complicated gender, and desperate desire for personal freedom, saw her and the life she'd built for herself as the thing I wanted. And her as my path toward getting it.

Before I met her, I'd found her interesting.

After I met her, I discovered myself in love for the first time.

So I did exactly what Oe told me to do. Worked myself into Cady's life, made myself invaluable to her, had her take me where her investigation took her. And then used her to kill all the Oldcity members of USAG present in that special meeting, and along with them, Danniz Oe.

She did what I could not do. Could not even think about doing.

She didn't know it. But she set me free.

Chapter Ten

WHEN I WAS FEDARA CONTEI

I'm good at math.

It is a blessing.

And a curse.

By the time Danniz Oe was dead, by the time Cady and Badger were getting ready to tell the man who'd hired them that they'd located his stolen spaceship, I could pinpoint both a best case and worst case for the point at which the population of Oe's contagiously spreading vampirism would wipe out humanity.

And I couldn't think of a thing to do to stop it.

But one of the things I discovered — in my incredibly invasive exploration of Cadence Drake's past — was that when she took her captain's exam, she'd earned the second highest score ever on the Suitability for Deep Space test. Which is also known as the Kartach Norgan test.

Turns out the same take-charge, assume responsibility, go-it-alone-to-get-the-job-done qualities that make people reliable under horrific pressure in space are also great qualities for allowing them to become dictatorial monsters if they choose careers in politics. Hence

Kartach Norgan, named after the original settled space dictatorial monster.

The test for this is so physically overwhelming and potentially destructive — it can actually kill the taker mid-test — that giving it has been outlawed in most "civilized" worlds. So even though there's a foolproof way to find out which people should never be given power over other people's lives, most would-be and actual politicians are never tested.

Taking your million-rucet pleasure cruiser through origami points using TransFold Navigation? Oh, yes. We can certainly kill a few people to make sure you get safely to the Moon of Prepubescent Sex Toys and back home again. So anyone — anywhere — who wants to become the captain of a Transfold Navigation ship that can jump across solar systems by folding through origami points *must* take the Kartach Norgan. Excuse me. The whitewashed name of that test is the Suitability for Deep Space — SDS — exam.

On average, sixty percent of those who who have completed the rigorous deep-space pilot training fail this final test. They are instantly disqualified from ever being Trans-Fold Navigation pilots, and limited to in-system jobs.

However, the forty percent who pass are instantly disqualified from ever being politicians. Ever. Why?

To give what follows some perspective, the average score on normal people subjected to this test is two to five percent. These folks are considered safe for society.

To be a TFN captain, you have to score better than forty — but if you score more than *twenty*, you're considered a megalomaniacal danger to humanity if put in charge of a government.

Cadence Drake had scored an eighty-nine on the test. It was surreal — the second highest score ever recorded.

Only one earlier student scored higher than that — a ninety-seven, which was the most terrifying thing I'd ever seen, and I'd been Danniz Oe's mind slave.

I could have used that ninety-seven scorer. But the taker of *that* test had disappeared. I both knew Cady and knew how to find her.

I knew what the problem was. Danniz Oe's Legend virus was spreading with exponentially accelerating speed.

But while I would probably score fairly high on the Kartach Norgan if anyone could force me to take it, I was no one's eighty-nine percent.

I could not see a path to solving the Legend disaster that was racing straight at us.

Cady's brain, however, would work in ways that mine couldn't. Kartach Norgan high-scorers land on their feet, figure out solutions when none are apparent, never ever *ever* give up until they're dead. And even Death generally has to take an army to stop them.

I didn't know how to get her on my side. I knew she'd seen me approach Oe before she killed him. I knew she'd seen me smile at him, whisper something to him. I knew she would think I'd betrayed her.

So if she saw me, she would try to kill me.

I managed to gain access to her ship using the Cantata-wide override pass I'd lifted from Danniz Oe's pocket right before Cady killed him. That pass was the reason I'd gone up to him during his demonstration of Legend II, smiled at him, stood beside him, touched him. When I touched him, I stole it.

The action didn't harm him. Didn't threaten him.

And because I was basically his business manager slave, having that override was something I knew I had to do in order to protect his investments.

I did not let myself think about why I would need to

protect those investments in the near future… But it turns out there's nothing built into Legend that forces you to try to save your owner when you know something else is going to kill him.

Just as she had to live, *I had to live.* I had to put her on the path to clearing the Legends from settled space, to getting humanity off the endangered species list.

So I was in the *Hope's Reward*, and had been waiting, hidden out of the way, trying to figure out how to get her to see reason, hoping she would work with me one last time when I heard her propose marriage to Badger. Propose settling down somewhere with the money they were going to get from the man who'd hired her and set her on the path to finding USAG, Peter Crane. She was talking about becoming domestic. Settling down. Raising a family.

Marriage and children would prevent her from finding a way to stop my kind of creature from spreading. From even discovering how bad the problem already was, and how much worse it was going to become.

Then her mother stepped out of a hiding place I hadn't noticed, moved into position in front of me, cast a little smile back in my direction, and whispered, "My kill, not yours."

Cady's mother wanted to kill her.

Lashanda had Cady at a disadvantage, and Badger was unarmed. Why the hell was Badger unarmed?

And then her mother did the unexpected. Told Cady that she and I had been working together, and that when I had suggested splitting Meileone with her, she'd killed me.

I was standing right behind her, just a bit off to one side, out of sight. And she knew it.

And she said *I was dead, and that she'd killed me.*

To this day I don't know what she thought that would accomplish.

Lashanda told Cady and Badger to go with her. She was going to get them off the ship, take them someplace private, kill them and make them disappear.

And then Badger did the stupidest, bravest thing I've ever seen. He shouted, drew an imaginary gun, dropped, rolled, pretended to fire.

He pulled Lashanda's focus away from Cady for a split second. Cady shot her mother full of AntiLegend.

Her mother shot wildly and took off one of Cady's legs — but the nice thing about lasers is that they seal when they cut. Cady would live.

Lashanda exploded all over the cargo bay. Not a problem for any of the three of us, because we were all three immune to Legend, being full of AntiLegend, the agent I'd had created so humanity could wipe out Legends like me.

Rule number one in creating the weapon that would kill you and everyone like you? *First, make sure it can't kill you.*

So even as Lashanda was trying to kill Cady, I shot and killed Badger. For humanity to survive, Badger couldn't. It was a terrible thing to do. And I swear it had nothing to do with me wanting Cady for myself, because… well… Cady thought I was already dead. And had been her mother's ally.

But that wasn't the point.

If Badger lived, Cady and he would settle down, start a family. Become soft and dull and content.

When I shot Badger, knowing that Cady would find out I'd been the one to kill him, I accepted that to push her into the mode that would set off the unstoppable Kartach Norgan juggernaut inside of her, that would set her on my trail and push her into discovering the Legend population explosion, I would have to live the rest of my eternity without her.

I knew she would know I'd killed Badger.

I knew by killing him I would become forever her enemy.

But to find my kind, she had to come after me. So I decided before I took the shot that I could live with that. I would lead her to the dangers, she would pursue. She would find what I knew, and because she was something that I am not, she would see a way to end the problem, if one could be found.

Love can be replaced. Rediscovered in someone else.

Trillions of human beings eliminate any dream that there is just one person in the universe who will be right for you.

Immortality gives you the chance to keep looking.

Unless, of course, something is wiping out humanity.

If humanity becomes extinct, your chances of finding love and the life you want to live are… none.

Chapter Eleven

TWO HOURS AFTER BAILEY'S POINT WON THE WAR...

Melie, captain of the *Longview*, was looking over the owner's request to rebuild the City of Furies on one of Bailey's inner planets when Mado Keyr came onto the bridge.

She rose, and he said, "You've seen it?"

"I haven't gone through everything yet, but I'm more than halfway."

"And?"

Melie considered being tactful, but decided against it. "This is the strangest proposal I've ever seen. I cannot figure out why you're pushing to do this. You're talking about making an exact duplicate of an existing city that is currently well hidden from its enemies — and the City of Furies still has many enemies, even if the Pact Worlds Alliance has had its teeth pulled. You're talking about putting this exact duplicate on one of the inner planets of Bailey's Point, where it will no longer be hidden at all." She shook her head. "I cannot imagine how people who are currently safely hidden from people who want them dead would consider moving from their current city to your duplicate."

The owner nodded. "Reasonable reservations. May I briefly borrow you from what you're doing?"

Melie stood, indicated that her second should take the captain's chair. Once he assumed command, she followed the owner.

When they were off the bridge, he said, "You need to understand the City of Furies, and why I'm proposing what I am. So I'm going to show you the part of the ship that only I have access to. From now on, you'll have access as well."

"This is something your captains take on as part of their duties?"

"No," he said. "Just you."

She considered that, bit her lower lip. Nodded. This, then, was part of the mystery of the ship. Part of all of those things none of the crew could ever speak about, could never question.

This was the one mystery she had not been able to solve in spite of her skills.

The "why" behind the vast dark deeps filled with countless men and women in suspended animation. The heavily armored ship core with No Entry signs and high security ident scans at every hatch… and possibly the comings and goings of people brought in by the owner who were never introduced to or identified for the crew, who disappeared into the ship for a time, then reappeared and left, never to be seen again.

He was leading her toward his quarters, though.

She looked over at him, her question in her one raised eyebrow, and he said, "I have access to things no one else on this ship has. And that access is convenient for me."

He took her into a dark general room, in which she

could see a desk, some chairs close to a large moleibond viewport out into space, stairs to her right, and a door in front of her and to the left.

"We're going that way," he said and pointed to the door.

He led.

She followed.

They stepped into a low, narrow corridor, followed it up a short flight of stairs, then down a long tight passage-way. If she'd been subject to claustrophobia, she would have panicked. As it was, she found herself uncomfortable. She tried to keep her bearings within the ship. She could tell she and Keyr were working their way along a hidden layer between the outer hull and what she knew had to be criminal storage, but at the point where they went up one gravdrop, zigzagged through a corridor that had to be working its hidden way into the ship's interior, and then up another gravdrop, she was lost.

They came out onto a balcony and into a vast open space filled with a massive floating sphere that glittered, glowed, pulsed with ever-changing lights.

"That's beautiful," she whispered.

He nodded. "It's my nightmare. My love. My passion. And now it has become the end of me."

Chapter Twelve

WHEN I BECAME WERIX KEYR

A massive amount of money was sitting in accounts all over settled space, growing. And I as Fedara Contei was its executor.

But I wasn't its inheritor. The man on all the records was Mado Werix Keyr.

So with Danniz Oe dead, if I wanted to free up that money, I was going to have to produce Werix Keyr.

I considered dressing up one of my victims who was a Legend because of me and modifying him to assume the identity of the wealthy man...

But look how well enslaving his victims had turned out for Danniz Oe.

The intelligent learn from history. They don't repeat it.

So I went back to Storm Rat, and I told the truth — most of it, anyway. Storm Rat and his people already knew of my underage prostitution disguised as mentorship when I was Tadra Amu and my origin as an infant born into the Living Saints cult, including my escape from slaughter at puberty as K-Eighty-Four.

I went back to them as Tadra Amu, escaped slave of

the dead Danniz Oe, skipped straight over my middling stay as StranP01, and melded the past they knew into the Fedara Contei ID I had at the time because StranP01 wasn't on record. However, I did note that in order to guarantee my permanent willing servitude, Oe had injected me with a body mod that, if it were altered in any way, would kill me. I explained that I needed to have them be careful working around those nanoviral changes.

So they were careful. They didn't dig, didn't pry into the story. They'd been able to verify my history both times, so they let me into their little world. While I was there, they treated me with reserved, careful kindness.

I kept to myself, kept my teeth to myself, spent every second that I could alone on my own little ship with my supply of stolen frozen blood.

They had *all* been slaves — Storm Rat and his associates and his allies. They had all lived their own horror stories, and they had no problem understanding that I didn't want to spend time with them. I just wanted to get fixed, get away... and they respected my privacy.

When I explained what I wanted and why — and I told them the absolute truth about this — it took them a week to deliver. During that week, I lived in orbit and ate only once — and was grateful that Oe had spent so much time and money decreasing the required frequency of feeding.

Storm Rat's team built a genderflip profile for me that would let me use my private Medix (or any public Medix) to change from Fedara Contei to Weyrix Keyr. The way they did it was clever. They embedded a Fedara Contei identity reju pod in the tip of my left index finger (I'm a lefty), and a Werix Key identity reju pod in the tip of my right one.

And they built an incredibly clever neural rewire

scheme that controlled handedness, so I didn't ever accidentally screw up and use the wrong ident.

They made Werix Keyr a natural right-hander. So when I genderflip, I automatically come out of the box presenting the correct finger for ident checks. The correct eye for optical checks. I don't have to think, to hesitate. I'm always just myself inside my skin.

I have a bit of numbness in both fingertips now, but in a society where demanding a bit of your blood and tissue to prove who you are is both mandatory and frequent, numbness has its benefits.

Able to be both Werix Keyr and Fedara Contei, I went on my way, with the few people discovered I actually trusted knowing more truth about me than anyone except Danniz Oe ever had.

And I discovered that was an oddly comforting feeling.

Every single step I'd taken to create Werix Keyr was, of course, illegal as all hell. But in most of settled space, even thinking unapproved thoughts is illegal. In those places, the only way to be one of the good guys is to be a criminal.

I spent a week jumping to different systems, doing a couple of random TFN jumps into undocumented systems just to lose my backtrail — worthwhile inconvenience because it protected Storm Rat and his people — and then presented myself as Werix Keyr with Danniz Oe's death certificate for each account that I'd created and hidden.

I walked away from that step inconceivably rich.

The Werix Keyr money was clean money. The instant Oe's death was confirmed, Danniz Oe's name came off the accounts and all sign that it had ever been there disappeared. That money became mine, with no sign that it had been associated with a monster.

With no history of how I'd made it, either.

The rest of Oe's holdings were problematic.

Werix Keyr had also been listed as the beneficiary on Oe's public accounts and purchases. I'd told him not to worry. I'd make up a phony name, give it a contact address that ID monitors would confirm, and add that to the accounts. He'd agreed.

So as Werix Keyr, I found myself the owner of a lot of terrible things.

Most I let sit, because they were infested by Legends like me, and I could not in good conscience allow those possessions and the monsters on them to pass into the hands of innocents.

Some I was able to unload because they were clean.

When I had done what I could to distance myself from Oe, I called home the most conservative of the hidden investments I'd been making for Danniz Oe — that ancient colony slowship I'd had refurbished as a Death Circus. This particular vessel had originally been built to transport five hundred thousand people and their few possessions and the seed tech that would build their colony on a new world. The ship had been filled with the bulky, primitive hibernation units of the time.

It was massive, ugly, sturdy, slow.

And it was haunted. If not by real ghosts, then by its own history.

It had been the hope of half a million people trying to escape the hell of repressive world government that Old Earth had become.

It had been the scene of mass genocide... and mass enslavement.

I tried to imagine half a million people being so desperate to escape the only home the species had ever known that they were willing to sell everything they owned, to pay the exorbitant fees to have their blood drained, to have their bodies filled with hibernation fluid, to have themselves flash frozen... and to then face centuries of travel locked in primitive freezer boxes just to have a chance to reach a place where they couldn't even be sure they would find a home.

The ship had been named *Long Winter Kind Spring*. Its winter had been short, though, less than fifty years. And its spring never came.

Following the discovery of origami folds and points by Isas Yamamoto, a number of labs perfected moleibonding techniques that created hulls capable of moving ships and the humans inside them through the tearing pressures exerted by the folds. Once humans could survive being squeezed through the origami points, nearly instantaneous point-to-point space travel opened up.

And criminals, always early in the adoption of new tech, plotted out where every slowship they could find would be in its passage. They gathered in bands, hit these rich, unarmed targets, freighted off the supplies that would have built and supported colonies and sustained them for their first hundred years... and then these inventors of space piracy systematically slaughtered the hibernating adult males and took the hibernating women and children to revive and sell as slaves.

I do not know of a single colony established anywhere by slowship survivors.

The funny thing is, there probably are several, but they're in solar systems without origami points — and thus free from any threat of space piracy.

They're safe from the worst that settled space has to offer — but out of reach of the best, too. And they're stuck — permanently stuck. Humanity grew into settled space in less than a hundred years because out past Pluto, humanity *had* an origami point, and when Isas Yamamoto located it, our door opened.

Those rare slowship colonists, wherever they might be, are survivors only because they have no door.

When I became Werix Keyr, in any case, I recalled my Death Circus from its route. At that point, I rechristened the *Long Winter Kind Spring* the *Longview*. It had already been moleibonded, fitted with TFN drives and the best in-system drives, already had a million of the best existing hibernation units installed — these less than a third the size of the primitive slowship units, so that a million of them fit easily into less space than those original units had required — taking up only the middle third of the ship. The back third at that time was empty.

At the point I went aboard, my ship held nearly a hundred thousand criminals in hibernation.

I kept the newly christened *Longview* off its route only long enough to add in a luxurious apartment suite for myself and to improve the accommodations for a small crew.

I did this because I had an idea — a dream — but it was something that would, I thought, take hundreds or thousands of years.

I wanted to create a culture of human beings who exported freedom the way Old Earth had exported its terrible ideas of top-down governance and the enslavement of the individual for the benefit of those who ran the government. People can escape planets, but they rarely outrun their unexamined assumptions, the primary of these being that the job of a government is to take care of its people.

Its people. Hold those two words in your head for a moment, and really think about them.

If the people *belong* to the government, rather than belonging to themselves, slavery is built right in.

For the first time in my life, I belonged to myself.

And I wanted to bring other people with me. To find slaves, free them, teach them to think for themselves, teach them self-reliance, encourage them to work for their own benefit and to never accept the idea that they needed to be made sacrifices to someone else's demands.

To give them a protected world in which to live — and then let them prove to all of settled space that a government answerable to and owned by its citizens, with humans whose unfettered freedom gave them a legal and inalienable right pursue their own dreams and desires in a society that understood freedom's value, would outperform every form of slavery humanity had invented.

As I said, I saw this taking thousands of years. And while I was immortal, I knew I would need time to figure out how to bring about the future I desired. The *Longview* held in storage the blood of all those nice clean criminals to keep me healthy while I figured it out.

At that point, I did not know that there were already escaped slaves out there hunting down slavers, killing them, and freeing their slaves.

I did not know that there were rebels hidden deep inside slaver governments working against those who demanded to be served.

I had not yet read the works of Bashtyk Nokyd.

Back then, the news of all these things was suppressed.

So with me aboard, the *Longview* resumed its Death Circus route with a fresh crew, and with me as a mysterious, damaged man who avoided all human contact and kept to his apartments. I made my money without interfering with the workings of the ship.

Chapter Thirteen

WHEN I WAS WERIX KEYR

Money makes money.

With Danniz Oe dead and my identity as Werix Keyr established, however, to use that money to fund my thousand-year plan to reintroduce human freedom, I had to have the backstory that permitted the right kinds of people — the ludicrously rich ones — to give me their money without question.

So even though I was living on the *Longview*, I purchased an ancient, grand home on the core PWA world Meileone, in the most prestigious city, Cantata, and in the best and most revered neighborhood — Oldcity.

The story Storm Rat had given me made me a direct descendent of one of the best Old Earth families. My lineage and massive fortune made it simple for me to keep to myself. I simply moved into that fine Oldcity neighborhood. I did not immediately refurbish the ancient home — refurbishing landmark buildings into flashy new buildings is the mark of the nouveau rich. I took on only a handful of servants to tend my grand home and rewarded them well for maintaining the house when I was away.

I did not try to meet anyone in Oldcity. I maintained my quiet reserve, funded the finer things in the city like the arts and sciences, continued to invest with an eye toward reliable, cautious growth.

Threw no parties, accepted only one invitation, and that one a personal, private invitation to a dinner with just Cantata's governor and a handful of his closest friends who had gathered specifically to meet me. To that party I wore a pressure suit with a rebreather, socialized little, and left early, noting that the gravity of the planet quickly tired me. The story I gave was that I had a degenerative neurological disease that did not respond to Medix treatments — there are a few such in the universe, and they are ugly. During that short dinner, I let it be known that I had to spend most of my time in space, in light gravity. On a ship I did not care to identify.

If you have enough money and have no interest in flaunting it, the things you say are taken at face value.

In that fashion, I had no problem passing myself as old money from Old Earth, which is as old as money can get.

During my three-month stay in the Oldcity house, I made conservative investments. And through my servants, I leaked a few facts I wanted to get into public circulation. The first was that I owned an ancient slowship, and that I'd had it fitted out as a Death Circus. The second was that I'd been the top bidder on seven original Sarling Fermee paintings. The third was my funding for the Oldcity Ancient Orchestra.

In such fashion, I established myself as an interesting investor, someone capable of growing money, someone capable of discovering new talent and bringing it to broader attention.

Death Circuses are very conservative investments,

because in these days of reju and body modding, the only thing more certain than death is taxes.

Meanwhile, investing in the work of Sarling Fermee proved me to be edgy. Willing to take chances. My bidding up of his works through several proxies working against me as the open bidder put him on the map.

Sarling Fermee was the inventor of alien hyperrealism. The artist whose work had made me want to be an artist. He had been my inspiration when I'd dared to dream of following in his footsteps, and even though that dream had not gone well for me, I still loved art. And his art. He was still alive, still working — and after my purchases, his future works would sell for more. I thought someday I would like to meet him.

I eventually did better than that. He now lives at 49 West Branch in the City of Furies. But how that happened is a story someone else will have to tell.

As for the orchestra? I enjoy classical music played by living musicians on analog instruments. Why not throw a publicly visible stream of rucets into that to keep it alive?

Meanwhile, my child self hiding down in her hole with the leaves pulled over her head had been working for my benefit when she pushed me in my Fedara Contei slave state to store all criminals who could not be sold for a hundred thousand rucets or more.

She was working, strangely enough, to save herself as well.

First, the sources of ethically obtained genuine human blood are few — but one of them is convicted Pact World Class B criminals, who do not fall under the protection of the Pact World Covenants.

Class A criminals — rapists, murderers, force-thieves, and others who have harmed others with intent, have very strict treatment and sentencing requirements.

But once off Meileone and back on the *Longview*, I finally got around to reading the "Operation of Your Death Circus Franchise" manual, and I discovered that Class B criminals, who have in almost all cases committed crimes not recognized by the Pact Worlds Alliance as major crimes, are treated under the "do anything you want with them as long as you don't kill them" rule given to all planetary franchises when they buy their licenses.

Class B criminals are almost always thought criminals — those who challenge the position of the people in charge. Thus, they are usually far more hated by their world's governments than Class A criminals.

On most franchise worlds, therefore, they are starved, tortured within an inch of their lives, and paraded before other citizen-slaves as examples of what happens to those who dare to think.

Once they are at Death's door (but not over it, because killing them is a primary prohibition in the franchise terms of ownership, for which a license could be revoked without recourse), they are sold for next to nothing to the next passing Death Circus.

From my manual, I discovered that the Death Circuses, which were required to purchase a percentage of Class B criminals at every location, were encouraged to take these thought criminals outside of Pact Worlds boundaries and dump them out the airlock.

So the sentence of Class B criminals was in reality to be tortured for as long as they could survive it, only to be murdered silently and conveniently away from any public eye.

Franchise colonies were terraformed and placed where out-of-mainstream religions and philosophies, theme vacation chains, and special-needs/special-desires resorts could operate away from mainstream culture. Where they could set up with their franchise's rules, then advertise for and get settlers who paid big fees to join them. These franchises, all guilty of deceptive advertising, became the biggest source of Class B criminals.

Franchise colonies were eyeballs-deep in regulations with oversight directly by the Pact Worlds Alliance and its crony inspectors. But the regulations were for the prevention of spread of disease, for the prevention of bad publicity for the franchise, and for the improvement of cash flow.

Buying a Class A criminal requires a massive amount of paperwork, because each one is a valuable commodity. They can be resold to the entertainment market, where they become gladiators or torture whores, or where they can be forced to do any of a thousand other terrible jobs. Better yet, the more horrible their crimes, the better the price the seller can get for them, because the worst of them can be auctioned for Public Execution if their crimes are horrible and entertaining enough to get the Pact Worlds' entertainment division interested in purchasing execution broadcast rights. The Good, Decent, Rich Class A citizens of the Pact Worlds like to have their nasty, dirty fun where proof of it can't follow them home. And they like to cheer on the screaming and blood of a good, gory execution now and then.

Class B prisoners require only the maintenance of an IDENT form and a DATE OF DEATH form. And Class B prisoners have never done anything that can be sold for broadcast or anything that can be pointed to as a real crime. They are the people who dare to have a sense of self, who dare to think that they have a right to live their lives the way they want. They're the folks who paid to emigrate to a new world where freedom was promised, only to discover that they'd paid to be slaves in a worse world than they'd left.

As thought criminals, Class B folks are unwelcome almost everywhere in settled space. Slavery in its many guises creates very nice lives for the few at the top, and whether these few are kings or government officials, those at the top survive only by locking down those at the bottom.

Kings and government officials alike want those below them to obey silently and without question — and if they dare to question, those at the top want them to die. However, in societies where forks record what their users eat and glasses monitor what their users drink, where servants and friends and even lovers constantly record the actions of the people in their lives, where everything watches almost everyone almost all the time, those at the top need to appear clean. To pretend to themselves and their slaves that they are Friends of the People.

When, as Fedara Contei, I instructed the crew of the Death Circus I purchased to store all criminals who could not be sold for a high return, I didn't know why the Class Bs were so cheap, so plentiful, or so easily disposable. I guessed that what they'd done was so horrible they could not be allowed to live, but that they had to be disposed of invisibly to prevent others from knowing such evil existed in the universe.

If you're a dictator perched precariously on top of a pyramid of slaves — and people start agitating for individual freedom — I suppose that's actually your belief.

In any case, the "Operation of Your Death Circus Franchise" handbook offered tips on ways to get top dollar for my Class A criminals. And suggested hiring one of their Recommended Helpers to find a nice origami point to a solar system with no planets, a dead sun, or another serious flaw, and then to always use that system to dump my Class Bs out the airlock.

Worlds with most Class As and Class Bs were listed in the handbook, along with percentages of Bs that had to be purchased to permit the buying of or bidding on Class As.

And then I discovered that the Beckenridge Colony of Living Saints was listed as one of the most profitable colonies in settled space.

That it had one citizen, the Saint.

That every other person on the world was a product: a Breeder, a Trained, Neutered Slave, or Class B — a disposal problem for the world's owner when he was done with that person.

And I froze.

I'd thought that I had genuine criminals in storage. I'd thought that I'd maintain them as unconscious, preserved, safe food storage for me. I was going to be — I thought — kinder to them than the other Death Circuses. I wasn't going to let all that ethically obtained blood go to waste out an airlock and into deep space.

But I discovered in that moment that everyone on Beckenridge had been a tool for the satisfaction of the Saint and those to whom the Saint rented out or sold his little-boy "products".

I had escaped that evil bastard's child-sex and child-disposal program on his legally franchised, working-within-the-letter-of-the-law private haven. But I might have been the only one who did.

I got cold.

Quiet.

And very, very angry.

Angry enough to buy the Saint's world from him for a hefty profit, then make to make sure he died hideously and secretly, wide awake, knowing exactly who I was and why he was dying at my hand. His death took a very long time.

Angry enough to take every single survivor off his world and put them in my Medixes until I figured out what to do with them.

Angry enough to see, for the first time, what the Pact Worlds Alliance really was. To see beyond my own nose, beyond my own pain, beyond my own self pity to the galaxy beyond, to the people trapped in situations they could not change, could not fix, and would not survive.

I was angry enough that I *finally* asked the question I needed to ask, which was simply this...

How do I use this vast fortune I've acquired, this ship that was just going to be my legal food source, and this franchise that gives me access to places most people don't even know exist, to stop slavery in all its many forms in settled space?

Chapter Fourteen

MELIE

"The end of you?" Melie asked.

"I'm dying today," Keyr said. "It's a necessary part of my life. I've found the people who can keep what I've created going, who can bring it into the real universe, who can protect it and nurture it and make sure that it stays true to its principles.

"From that," he said, "I can finally release my pain, step away from the anguish of the life I have been dragging myself through, day by agonizing day, for years. I can let go, embrace the darkness, cease to exist." He looked at Melie, and she could feel the power and intensity of his gaze even through the darkened faceplate of his heavy shipsuit.

"My invention," Keyr said. "It's the City of Furies. And every slave we've taken in since I began building it lives there. We have almost a million people in the city now — living and working — and the ship's storage can hold no more."

She stared at the sphere, which she guessed took up the entire back third of the *Longview*.

"The City of Furies is virtual?"

Keyr nodded.

Then the truth hit her. "The PWA attack. If it had hit the *Longview*, it would have destroyed the City of Furies…"

"The city needs to be real," he said. "A real place with real protection. It needs to be a destination people can come to of their own free will. It needs to have families, children, the dynamic of real, physical human interaction. I have given it as much reality as I can, but every human being in the city is trapped inside a specially designed Medix that allows communications with others through the sphere — but only mimics human touch. And cannot duplicate the creation of children, or aging, or change. So everyone in there is always thirty, and for people who have been in there since the beginning, the fact that they do not change is starting to be a troubling mystery."

Melie looked at the magnificent sphere. "What do you want me to do?"

"I want you to help me bring the City out of its prison and into a real world. I want you and Shay to make it live."

Chapter Fifteen

HEROG

Herog told the other folks working with him, "This is a deep, complex virtual reality, operating in some version of real-time, connected back to physical reality in such a way that you can communicate with it, can send out your broadcasts and reports, so that new people can come here — but there's something between the outside and the inside, between all of Settled Space and this complicated program, that filters out the would-be spies and killers and traitors before they can do you any harm."

"If we're safe here, why does Mado Keyr want to take the City of Furies from virtual to tangible? If he's already managing to keep everyone who can do us harm out of the city, why put us at risk?"

The owner had told him that during the battle they'd just won, for the first time the City of Furies had been at risk of annihilation.

Not that it had been found. Just that it had been at risk of annihilation. Had stated that it had no defenses, and had never had, because it had not needed them.

It had to be housed somewhere in the immense *Longview*. And now Keyr — whoever Keyr really was — had realized that he couldn't keep the entire population of a city inside his ship, dragging them from danger to danger, leaving them vulnerable.

He was looking for a way to protect them away from himself.

A way to give them real lives.

Herog realized he was still on the *Longview*.

He sat down.

"We're all on his ship, and my friends and I just barely managed to keep Bailey's Point and the *Longview* safe. Mado Keyr could have lost everything, and this magnificent city and every one of you would have blinked out of existence without ever knowing you'd been in danger. This is why the City has to be real. Why it has to be built and why all of you have to be moved into it. This is why it currently has no defenses, and why it must have them."

He rested his elbows on the table, rested his face in his hands, and thought.

"But Keyr has already built the defense it needs. He just doesn't realize how good this system is."

He looked back up at them and grinned. "I know how we can protect the City of Furies without militarizing Bailey's Point or building the monster we fear."

Chapter Sixteen

WERIX KEYR

The poor, the downtrodden, the slaves held captive by governments and the slaves in chains alike have always told stories of a place where people are free.

All slaves have always imagined that there is some hidden wonderland where, if they could only get there, they could become the masters of their own destinies.

The stories are always the same.

Somewhere, there is a shining city, walled and glorious, protected by brilliant technology, by its hidden location, and by the ferocious citizens who guard their lives and each other's.

Somewhere.

The slaves always have their theories, and the masters, who know the stories are wishes unburdened by any truth, let them talk.

Some call this shining city Freeland, but there are half a hundred real worlds named Freeland in various world alliances, and every single one generates their version of citizen-slaves and Class-B criminals.

Some call this mythical world Godshome, but there are many, many colony worlds settled by the religious that are named Godshome, and those repress their citizens in other ways.

The stories about the mythical City of Furies are the only ones that stand without a real-universe namesake.

Something about that name and about the story behind it has made the slave collectors wary of using it for their new colonies.

Unlike Freeland or Godshome or the other tales of utopias, the City of Furies has never been described as a place where everyone is rich and no one has to work — and that, I think, is why no slaver has built a settlement with that name.

The myth of the City of Furies only began circulating sixty or so years earlier, and from the beginning, it was this: The City of Furies is a place where people choose their own work, work hard, grow rich making things other people want to buy, buy things other people make. People create, invent, innovate. And all of them pay their own way. In this city that tolerates no oppression, no slavery, no classes, the lowliest freed slave can become rich and admired, and no one will stand in his way, or hold him down because his parents were slaves, or he was marked Class E.

In the stories, this one city is a place where religion is tolerated but never mandated. Where various schools of thought are tolerated but never mandated. Where differences of opinion are accepted, where the rule of law stands above a slide to tyranny, where the rich have no more or better rights than the poor.

I thought the City of Furies was pure fantasy — the dream of those few slaves who did not want to switch their lots to become the masters of slaves.

And it was the best fantasy I'd ever heard of. I didn't think such a place could be made real.

Then I found Bashtyk Nokyd, and started reading his works.

And discovered that he'd written a novel titled *Aari in the City of Furies.*

The hero escaped from slavery, rescued his friends and loved ones, led them to a tiny world well away from the people who had once owned them, and he and his companions forged a code of conduct and a philosophy that gave them all equal rights under law, but that required that they earn those rights by bearing full responsibility for their own lives.

Responsibility for their own lives.

That, I thought. That was how people proved who they were. By owning their lives fully, by having nothing to prop them up but their own effort and the efforts of those with whom they traded, and by accepting the consequences of their own actions.

If only I could build such a place, I thought.

And then, sitting on one of the biggest piles of money in settled space, I thought, *I could build such a place.*

As a test.

In secret.

Set it up so that it ran on the rules Nokyd had developed. Make sure it did not fall prey to corruption, graft, favoritism, cronyism...

By building it inside a virtual reality, I could both protect the people inside the city who valued their chance at freedom, and identify and remove those who were looking for something for nothing, or who were criminals looking for prey.

Those people stored in my Medixes who were genuine monsters — their blood I could drink without remorse.

But I would never assume someone was a monster because he or she had been called one on a slaver world, had been sentenced by slaver law, had been sold by slave masters.

I promised myself that every human being within my care would have the opportunity to prove his or her character, to earn true freedom in a place where the individual was the pinnacle of humanity.

The people who were like the child I had been on Beckenridge, the child who wanted to be free to be myself, to find the life I wanted — those people I could give an opportunity to become their best selves inside the safe walls of a virtual City of Furies.

Through Storm Rat, I found a purely virtual AI who was interested in taking on the project. The AI had to agree to step out of common circulation, wall itself away from all outside communication within the *Longview*, and help me design both the protective barriers that would keep the City of Furies safely hidden, and the connections that brought each person in one of my storage units into the city. The two of us decided that the city needed to start small, and that each of the first people in it had to be treated as a new settler, given a few basic colonization tools and the chance to use those tools to build a piece of the city he or she would inhabit.

We set the time cycle to one virtual year per physical day. Started with a hundred colonists, and a charter that spelled out Bashtyk Nokyd's Rules of Human Freedom. Each hour of the first seven days, we added access to a hundred new settlers, and improved the settlement tools, and made sure we gave them the "history of the settlement" and trained them in Nokyd's Rules of Human Freedom.

By the end of the first week of real time, we had all of

the criminals who had been in storage longest inside the city — and who were willing to work within Nokyd's rules — settled. The earliest in had been living in the growing city for seven virtual years. And they were all thriving.

Nokyd's Rules worked.

The first of which is simply, "To keep all humans free from oppression, no one rides through life for free."

It was a terrible shock to some of those in my hold who had been brought up to believe that they deserved to be carried on the work of others because their lives had been hard, or because they had been slaves and now wanted to own slaves.

About a quarter of new immigrants to the City of Furies requested transfer following their first Immigrants' Orientation class, where they were informed that they had to find a paying job in their first month in the settlement, and also notified that they would have to pay for everything they needed. That they would be required to work, to create, to remain active participants in building the city to stay in the city. That nothing was or ever would be free.

Several successful inhabitants would come in to talk to them, and explain that even though they had become massively wealthy, to remain inhabitants and citizens, they were required to invest in the city and remain active participants in its growth and success.

Another fifteen percent washed out in the first month because they refused to look for work, refused to accept responsibility for their own lives.

They were removed from the virtual reality.

Through the years, I ran more than a million Class A and Class B criminals through the virtual reality program. I discovered to my dismay that vast numbers of people want something for nothing, and are willing to see others enslaved so they can have that.

I was heartened, however, to discover that over half of the people who'd been rescued by *Longview*, when they found themselves in the orientation room of the City of Furies, understood where they were, hugged each other or wept for joy or kissed the floor in gratitude.

And then they stood up straight, walked out into the city, and started building their lives.

They worked one job, or two. Saved money, rented rooms, paid for education, learned skills, offered services, built products, built infrastructure, created new businesses.

Some grew rich. Those invested in buildings, or research into how to improve the city, or explored improvements to technology. Some developed products that answered needs far beyond the City of Furies and exported their goods while remaining the owner-operators of those businesses. Some pursued second passions and became writers or artists or musicians or inventors and started exporting their work throughout the galaxy.

But the fact was presented to every prospective citizen that the City of Furies was a city that worked. There were many rich people in the city — and more with every new infusion of immigrants.

There were no *idle* rich.

People who would have been nothing but frozen food for me — had I not discovered the truth — instead built Bashtyk Nokyd's City of Furies. They invented massive breakthroughs in technology, wrote entire bodies of passionate fiction and nonfiction, made magnificent art and music, created a deeply embedded city-wide culture of individual independence and individual pride in accomplishments earned.

By having the inhabitants self-select for willingness to work, and by creating a culture that rewarded them for investing in themselves and pursuing their passions as a way to create work they loved, the city became the place I yearned to inhabit.

The people of the city loved who they became, and made the rule of the city the motto of the city.

The City of Furies: *The City that Works.*

The problem, of course, was the *other* people. Not the Class A Criminals who failed to take the chance they were given to build new lives. Those I could sell for profit or keep and use as food.

No. The problem was those people who self-selected as "want to own slaves, want to have other people pay for my existence, want to ride for free on the backs of those I force to carry me."

I did not want to dump them out the airlock.

I did not want to use them as food.

I did not want to sell them as slaves.

But I did not want to store them at my expense. Did not choose to fill up berths in my hold that were being hooked into the city with people who had designated themselves "want to be useless."

So I came up with an alternative.

Chapter Seventeen

WERIX KEYR

The urge to reproduce is a deep part of most people. We — and I do include myself in this number — yearn to pass on our genes, to create new versions of ourselves. To have children.

The City of Furies, being virtual, has no way to create children, because the citizens of the city are real, but their bodies are trapped in suspended animation. They do not age, they do not die… and they cannot breed.

But they still yearn.

So my Furies who have embedded themselves deeply in the culture and who have proven they understand why "no one rides for free" is the core that keeps the city alive are given the opportunity to "foster newborns."

This is something my AI and I came up with as an alternative to simply selling off the people who refused to adopt the Furies' culture.

People who were too damaged by their previous lives to move on — those who had endured horrific torture or the loss of people they loved deeply, or other traumas that made them not care whether they lived or died — along with people who saw owning slaves as their just repayment for having been slaves, and all Class A criminals in my hold were given three chances to become citizens of the city.

They were assigned two parents who got a new "infant" at least two virtual years after their previous one, and who raised these people as members of virtual birth families. The damaged, the criminal, and those with a sense of entitlement all retained their memories — because to erase their memories would have been to murder them — but they started their lives over with infant bodies that aged in what felt like real time to them. They experienced being born, being raised in loving families, being taught the Furies' culture and the history behind it. They received love, attention, education that focused on helping them discover and build on skills and passions that could form the backbone of rewarding careers, and were introduced to other children their own ages in tiny communities of ten to fifteen families in separate virtual realities outside of the city.

They were being tested, and each test lasted until the individual reached adulthood, was given autonomy with no sign of oversight, and then demonstrated who he or she had truly become.

Or who demonstrated earlier the intent to live the new life as badly as he or she had lived the old one.

Most of my people, given these opportunities, became hardworking, passionate creators inside the City. They remembered the pain their first lives had been filled with, but they no longer held on to it as a reason for revenge or as proof of their right to abuse others as they had been abused.

Those who were able to overcome the obstacles that prevented them from fitting into the City of Furies on their "immigrant" attempt made up the bulk of the rest of my human cargo.

A surprising number of people who had been career criminals found themselves joyful citizens of the City.

As did a decent number of people who had previously wanted to ride for free.

The others?

Well, I was operating a Death Circus, and I did have to make a certain number of sales to keep my Death Circus looking legitimate.

Those career criminals who proved they preferred crime to work (armed robbery being popular) — but who did not commit pedophilia, rape, torture, or murder in their family tests — I sold to the buyers who had found uses for such people.

Those in my possession who repeatedly demonstrated their desire to force others to do what they wanted so they could do nothing, I sold to worlds that bought slaves.

Those who had proven themselves irredeemable monsters, who when given caring families still committed rape, torture, pedophilia, or murder, I *kept*.

I found them both tasty and entertaining.

I do my best to be a good and honorable monster, but I am not a *nice* monster. I have needs, and sometimes I need to... play.

Chapter Eighteen

MELIE

The owner stood with his back to Melie, staring up at a crystal sphere that hung suspended in the center of the back third of the vast *Longview*.

Curls of light ran through the sphere, blue and gold and green, and darkness pulsed and shimmered in liquid sheets that fell up, down, sideways.

It was the most dizzying thing she had ever seen that did not include folding wide awake through an origami point.

"That," the owner said, "is the City of Furies."

Melie simply nodded, and kept her mouth closed so she didn't look like a slack-jawed idiot.

This was the owner's secret — the one she *hadn't* known. This was the thing he'd created, that he'd made real in a universe where *freedom* was a buzzword used for pulling in suckers and rubes and selling them to the highest bidder.

This was the strong thread of goodness she'd felt in him, the reason she'd trusted him.

In her gut, she'd felt the strength and the honorable

nature that drove the twisted and terrifying man. She had sensed this core of integrity, of genuine goodness, of passion for something so right and magnificent and wonderful — and so inconceivably complex and enormous — that she could not imagine what had driven him to create it.

All she had was the proof hanging before her that he had.

And she admired... loved... him for this incredible construct, this salvation for humans who had been slaves and who had been slated for death by being shoved out an airlock.

"Why?" she asked him. "You got away clean. You made yourself rich. You could have done anything. Why did you bring the best myth in the universe to life?"

He turned and looked at her. Raised an eyebrow.

"You know my past?"

She shrugged. "You know who I am. You know what I do. I did not intend to pry, but in the course of investigating those who were working to destroy us, I discovered those who had personal reasons for pursuing you. I know pieces of your past. Probably not the whole thing. But I know you were Tadra Amu. I know how you became Werix Keyr."

"That's probably more than I would have chosen to tell you."

"I assumed that. Kept it to myself. It was no one's business but yours, and had I not fallen over it while uncovering the secrets of those who attempted to overthrow Bailey's from the inside, I would not even have seen it."

He nodded, his eyes behind the faceplate of his suit unreadable as he studied her.

"So what do you think?"

"I think," Melie said, "that you are the most incredible human being I have ever known."

"I'm not human. Not anymore."

Melie laughed. "A body mod that you paid to have revised to make you less rather than more dangerous, from which you have had obligatory feeding, nanoviral bite-to-blood contagion, and lineage enslavement removed leaves you far more human than you care to admit."

She stopped laughing, though, as he froze. Stared at her unblinking, and she realized that he had truly not known how much she'd discovered.

"And you know that because...?"

"Because your enemies — many of whom share variants of the Legend body mod — investigated you thoroughly. Tracked your money and what you spent it on, tracked the people you contacted in various modding communities, tortured and killed some in order to get details. They lost your trail when they collided with someone even more cautious with you, but prior to that, they were very thorough. They concluded that you were looking for immortality without the side effects."

"Yes," he said. "Because I thought I would have to live forever to protect the *Longview* and its greatest secret. My city. Now I know that I can safely die and rid the universe of this horror that I am, and you and Shay will carry on. Bring the city out of virtual, give the citizens real lives, protect these people — these magnificent, creative, brave people who dared to build themselves into the best versions they could imagine of who they wanted to be. I'm showing you this now, because I'll die today, and this city will belong to you."

Chapter Nineteen

HEROG

Herog said, "It's simple. The city is built inside a vast terraforming dome. The entrances will have to require a Medix scan for anyone entering or leaving. That's standard procedure for any enclosed biome. In the three to five minutes the scan takes, Keyr's AI checks all returning citizens for alterations done without their consent — like the neural rewiring that led to Bashtyk Nokyd's death — and removes them.

"For prospective immigrants, it uses the exact process it's using now, whatever that might be."

Derna said, "But we don't know what that process is."

"We don't need to," Herog told her. "You are living inside the proof that it works. The proof isn't that no one has died here, or more importantly, has been born here. That was the proof that the place is virtual. It's that there have been no attempts to destroy the city or kill anyone. No one sent here to slaughter or destroy has been able to make an attempt, even if the attempt would have proved futile. No one intending harm has been able to enter the city."

Mecklen said, "That's invasion of privacy. This city cannot be the city it has become if it does not honor the rights of its citizens. And to dig through their minds to find intent, even if that intent is evil, is an invasion of privacy, of search without warrant, of everything that has already taken the rest of settled space in every imaginable wrong direction."

Herog nodded. "Returning citizens won't be searched. They'll simply be checked to make sure they were not tampered with or programmed to do things they would not do of their own free will."

"Then…" Mecklen began.

Herog held up a hand to stop him. "Immigrants who wish to become citizens cannot claim the rights of citizens. They must pass the test to prove they can live as citizens in this place before they are allowed to enter. The test is simply to get in the Medix and meet the AI."

"But their rights…"

"No one has a right to murder. No one has a right to rape, or a right to molest, or a right to torture, or a right to enslave. No one has a right to use force against any non-consenting innocent, and there will be those who are sent here to do those very things. The City of Furies will be under attack from the moment its location becomes known. It will have Bailey's army to protect it from military attack within its system. Not an army made to conquer, to go adventuring, to bring back loot and slaves. Not an army used to force the rest of settled space to adopt the City's path, for this is a path that cannot be followed by force. So the army must be made up of citizens who volunteer to serve for a time because they understand the value of what they're protecting."

"What if they won't volunteer?"

"Then what they claim to want to keep safe isn't worth saving."

"But the immigrants who are coming here to live better lives?"

"They'll pass the test as each of you did. But among them will be those sent to destroy the city, to cause chaos, to slaughter people who have already become known throughout settled space for their creation, for their honor, for their talents, for their joy. That the citizens of the City of Furies started as slaves and rose to greatness is already an affront to slave owners — whose sole claim to the right to enslave is that those who are owners are superior human beings, and those who are slaves are good for nothing better. The triumph of the citizens of the City of Furies is a threat to slavery. And the price of freedom is eternal vigilance. So no one may become a citizen who has not met the AI, gone through the test each of you went through before you were brought here."

Derna said, "There was no test. I was bought as a Class B criminal, I fell asleep, I woke up in the Immigrant Center, got my orientation, found a place to live, found a place to work." She shrugged.

Mecklen said, "Yeah. Same story for me."

"For you, that was the test," Herog said, "as it was for me. But that's not all there is to it. What happened before we woke up in the Immigrant Center?"

"Hah. Interesting." Liam said, "I remember another life before this one. I have not thought of it for years, and over time my memories of it fell away from lack of use... but I remember. I was a pirate in this other life. Was captured after I raided the wrong enclosure and killed the wrong people. Was sold to a slaver, was sent to a slave world, and I killed the owner of that world in an attempt to escape, which made me a Class-A criminal.

"I was purchased by a Death Circus. And then… Then I was being born. As an infant. Into a family.

"And that first life began to feel like a bad dream. I had two older brothers, an older sister, and a younger sister. And I learned math, and science, and engineering. It was a happy childhood, and then I came here, where my younger sister is a musician, where my brothers are — well, you know them. And my parents are still back on the farm. I go to visit them sometimes, but they have other children now." A tiny smile crossed his face. "And they're no older, but then… no one is."

Herog said, "That's how he does it."

The others looked over at him.

He said, "Those who need it are given a chance to start over. To be different. To make different choices, to choose better paths. Those who choose to change for the better come here. Those who don't…? I don't know what the owner does with those, but the fact that Liam is here and has family and friends and a life that matters to him is proof that the system gives people opportunity. The fact that you respect him enough to bring him into this process speaks well of you, of him, and of the justice built into the path to citizenship here."

He sat down, looked at Liam, Mecklen, Derna.

"The process Keyr is using works."

Chapter Twenty

WERIX KEYR

Melie stood behind me only because I turned my back on her.

I blinked the tears from my eyes, steadied myself. I was doing what I had to do — and the universe would be better off without me.

"Shay," Melie said behind me, "you don't have to kill him."

I froze, my breath caught in my chest. I turned slowly, not certain what I would find. Just knowing what I could *not* find...

And Melie was alone, staring at me. Just me.

"That's the secret I already knew," she said softly. Looking at me.

"How long?"

"Since right before you promoted me to captain. I've been waiting this whole time for you to tell me. But I suspected early on who you were, and have known for sure since the day you made me captain. Not just who you are, but what you are."

And I asked her, "How?"

"I suspected because you and Keyr were never in the same room together in sight of anyone—"

"Security precaution—" I said reflexively, and saw her eyebrow raise. I gave her an embarrassed little smile and shrugged.

"Then, after the on-deck crew was massacred, when the gravdrop was off and I made it up the ladder, I ran into you. You'd been in an explosion, you were naked, you were visible bones held together by meat and skin that was growing back fast, you were drinking the blood of the pirates to feed yourself. The skin of your face and skull was mostly burned off. But when you turned away from me, you had a flap of skin dangling from your skull down the back of your neck. The hair hanging from that flap was red, curly, waist-length. You were also missing male genitals, but that I would have overlooked because of the explosion. You were forming yourself into Keyr — forming yourself as male. By the hair, though — I knew you were Shay."

I stood staring at her. "You went to bed with me. Slept with me. A lot."

"I did."

"You knew what I was."

"I did."

I took a deep breath, stared at her and whispered, "Are you insane?"

She chuckled. "Possibly. But I knew both who and what you were, and even before the day you made me captain, enough of your history had landed in my lap, gathered by your enemies, that I understood why they were your enemies. If you were the devil, you were the devil on my side of the battle." She shrugged, and one corner of her mouth tipped upward. "Besides, I was in love with you —

at least with you as Shay — and I was willing to be a little stupid to have you."

I stripped out of the suit. Stood there before her, naked and male, and said, "And this?"

"You are who you are. All the parts, all the time. I'm not like you, and I'm not drawn to the Keyr part of you, but I don't think I need to be. You don't have to kill off a part of yourself for me. Keep Keyr. Use him however you want. Just save Shay for me."

Chapter Twenty-One

CADY

The little boy made it through.

Was being held by his mother in the room where the hostages were gathered, didn't see her. But Cady saw him and breathed a little easier.

The pang — that she still didn't have a child of her own — was fresh and sharp. She didn't introduce herself. She was happy to know he was all right, and that he still had a mother.

She...

Well, right then she had someplace else she needed to be.

She pulled rank as a friend of Wils Bailey to get out of the hostage debrief, and raced to her little apartment, pounding through the corridors of Bailey's Station, not looking around, not caring about anything but getting home. She needed to know that Herog was all right. But when she got home, he wasn't there.

An enormous crate filled with genuine RexSurvyve cookies sat on the floor of the apartment beside the table, which held a holo dot that showed Cady in the restaurant with the woman who'd been going to teach her how to bake RexSurvyve cookies.

She watched it. Saw that the friendly baker had also been taken hostage. She closed her eyes. Dragged herself back to the present, back to *this* moment, when she was safe at Bailey's, where Herog was missing or dead but his people had won their battle against the biggest and deadliest fleet of warships ever gathered.

She brought herself back to the gift he'd left for her.

Took out a Golden Almond Caramel and read the instructions.

In case of emergency, fix things first. Then open this packet, eat, and enjoy. You're going to be all right. — Contents, one Big Cookie.

She'd done everything she could to fix things. Had gotten back alive. Was where he could find her. But there wasn't going to be any Herog ever again, was there?

She took a bite of the cookie, thinking of his message to her. *You're going to be all right.*

She would.

Eventually.

This was her one life, and she would not throw it away, no matter how little it mattered to her at the moment.

She walked over to the apartment window, stared out at the black of space. It went on forever, and he was nowhere in it.

"Not even going to say hello?" the voice she knew she couldn't be hearing said from behind her.

She turned and he was there, filling the doorway, scarred and fierce and grinning.

"Herog!" She raced over to him. "You're alive."

"And so are you," he growled, and folded her into his arms.

He picked her up, spun her around, laughed happily.

"We're both alive," he said, "and we won."

"I saw part of the fight while I was hanging in that bubble waiting for rescuers to cut me out. I didn't know you were in it. My captors told me you were dead."

Herog said, "I needed them to think that, so they wouldn't kidnap you — but then they kidnapped you while I was killing myself off. I saw you come through in that bait ball during the first part of the invasion. I knew you might not make it — but before the fight, we did everything we could to make sure every hostage survived."

"How many hostages and rescuers died?"

Herog said, "Fourteen. Two hostages, two rescue teams, and part of a third that was too close to one of the balls that exploded. The teams were amazing. Keyr's people were brilliant and focused and incredibly well trained. He brought in some spectacular folks to help us."

"Keyr?" Cady asked.

"The same person with whom I have been — for what felt like eternity because I wanted to be here with you — working out the way for the City of Furies to move to one of Wils' planets. We need to go see Wils, by the way, to tell him he needs to sell Keyr the best one for a lot of money.

She looked up at him and said, "Want one of my cookies? You can have the whole thing."

He laughed. "Just this once, yes. I'd love to have a whole one."

So she handed him a Double-Butter Chocolate Chip, which was the very best kind.

And said, "I really need to learn how to make those."

He told her, "You'll be able to. Your friend the baker survived too. I checked on my way home."

Chapter Twenty-Two

SHAY

For the first time in my life, I'm whole. I am a complete human being, known completely by one other human being. Accepted for who and what I am.

Melie knows the whole story now. But she knew most of it already.

She chose to be with me in spite of the truth that she knew. The truth I never dared tell anyone, the truth I would have tried to kill off a part of myself to hide.

For the first time in my life, I *feel* human, inside and out. Not wrong, not broken.

I would say *not monstrous*. But I kept Keyr. I still have uses for him.

The City of Furies is a real place. Building it cost so much that I nearly outran my money. I hired every one of Wils Bailey's army of moleibonders who would work with me, and had them duplicate exactly the virtual City of Furies — which was tricky.

Because my people — no, *their own* people now — are so immensely creative, so driven, so passionate about their work and their lives, I had to pause the entire virtual reality, snapshot it and everyone in it, then hand off to Wils' people. I kept virtual reality paused at that exact spot so that the moleibonders could use the holographic records of the city in its state at the exact instant its citizens would return to it. The exact instant they left.

The zero-plane extruders created perfect duplicates of every structure, including those that were incomplete and being built. I had every article of clothing duplicated in place, every in-progress creation made real, duplicated every item owned down to the pen strokes in physical journals. The process for doing this had never been simple, but over the years that I'd been working for the citizens of the city, I'd built enormous deep-space facilities to fabricate in the real world the art and tech that they were creating in the virtual world, to sell what they were creating for them, and to invest the profits for them, so that those who became rich in the virtual world were rich in the real world too.

The citizens of the City of Furies became the beneficiaries of that process.

And then I tried to figure out a story — because there was no way I could move people from the middle of their virtual conversations to the same spots and the same words in interrupted conversations, without the break in reality being apparent.

In the end, I decided that the best I could do was to tell them the truth. That the city had been under attack. That everyone had been successfully rescued. That a small number of those folks who had volunteered to go into the real world to fight the Battle of Bailey's Point had died in the real world but were being restarted from their save points inside the city, without the memories of their service — but also without their deaths.

I paid to have every single citizen moved in the hibernation pods to their analog homes, put into medixes there, given simultaneous reju to make sure they were all as healthy as they could be. I worked with the city's AI to wake all of them simultaneously.

And spoke to all of them from inside their own homes at the same time. I had no great words for them. All I had was this.

"You built something amazing that was hidden away," I told them. "That only a select few could ever reach. The City of Furies was tucked inside a virtual reality, but everything you created now exists in the real world — and so do you.

"If you want to start families, you can.

"If you want to leave the City, you can.

"If you want to return to the rest of Settled Space, you can.

"It has been my honor and joy to see you prove the truth of Bashyk Nokyd's words: 'Great human beings are not born in great houses, or from great families. Great human beings beings create themselves one choice and one action at a time.' You are great human beings, and you are a beacon lighting the darkness. Live with joy."

Melie and I have a place in the City, private, quiet, a bit apart. We'll vacation there.

But for now at least, the sky is full of stars, and the stars are full of slaves, and we can yet find and rescue many of those who are like we were.

Someday I'm sure we'll want to settle into the City. Create a family of our own. Breathe the air of freedom. Walk the streets in the morning as the sun rises, and see all around us the faces of people glad to be building their lives, building their dreams; people who don't fear work, and who are working to build a city that is the proof to all of settled space that people achieve most and best when they are free to choose their own roads, and when they are fully responsible for the consequences of their own actions.

But for now — and if we can conquer death, forever — our true home is wherever we are together.

Afterword

This series began as my tribute to the *Canterbury Tales*, which when I was about seventeen introduced me to the reality that people in the far past were real human beings — pompous, funny, kinky, weird, stuffy, strange. Through Chaucer's work, I got to see a wonderful cross section of society, pinned brilliantly to the pages and saved so that hundreds of years later, I could meet people he saw every day. And recognize in them people *I* saw every day.

(The version of the book I had in high school had the Middle English version on the left page and the modern English translation in prose on the right. I worked my way through both.)

Chaucer made those people real to me, and by doing so, brought a time and place that had vanished from the face of the earth back to life.

And I thought, *Wouldn't it be cool to do that? To gather a group of strangers from another time together, to put them into a place where they had to deal with each other and depend on each other, to show readers their lives, what mattered to them... to make them live?*

In my case, I put my pilgrims on a spaceship in the

future, because people will still be people tomorrow, and beyond that. Will still be strange and weird, still pompous and funny. Will still think, dream, desire, love. Will still matter to themselves and to each other.

The Owner, the *Longview*, the folks at Bailey's, the citizens of the City of Furies — all of them touched my life, grew out of my past and my present, asked me questions as I was falling asleep at night, and gave me answers as I sat down to write the next day.

Some of these folks have been with me since before June of 2014, when I finished the first draft of *Enter the Death Circus*. That was the original title of *Born from Fire*, the first episode.

So what happens next?

From here, Melie and Shay get their "happily ever after."

Herog and Cady go back to work.

The folks on Bailey's Irish Space Station…

I don't know. I love BISS. And there are so many stories in there waiting to be told.

So many stories. So little time.

But while I like to write in my other worlds outside this universe, Settled Space is the place that feels like home to me. The place I want to keep coming back to after I've gone vacationing elsewhere.

I hope you find a home in this universe, too.

Holly Lisle
November 7, 2018 at 12:10 PM

Acknowledgments

My Bug Hunters

My deepest thanks to the folks who, when invited with no warning to bug-hunt this final *Longview* story on a ridiculously short deadline, said *Yes,* jumped in, and hit their deadline.

This story is way less buggy because of them:

Vanessa Wells
Kim Lambert
Tuff Gartin
Greg Miranda
Linda Sprinkle
Linda Niehoff

Any remaining errors, of course, are just mine.

My Patrons at Patreon

The following folks are currently funding me to write fiction for an hour a day five days a week.

They are the reason *The Longview Chronicles* are now complete.

My patrons in this episode are in Alpha by First Name order because of a series of events that started with me dousing my keyboard in coffee this morning, which resulted in me having to work on a wrong and not friendly computer…)

Adelaida Saucedo
Alex G. Zarate
Alexandra Swanson
Alicia Mayo
Amy Fahrer
Amy Padgett
Amy Schaffer
Anders Bruce
Angelika Devlyn
Anna Bunce
Anna K Payne
Ava Fairhall
Barbara Lund
Becky Sasala
Betty Widerski
Beverley Spindler
Beverly Paty
Bonnie Burns
Brendan Fortune
C. L. Roth
Carolyn Stein
Cassie Witt

Cat Gerlach
Catherine Ellison
Cathy Peper
Charlotte Babb
Chris Langston
Chris Muir
Christine Embree
Claudia Wickstrom
Connie Cockrell
Cynthia Louise Adams
Dan Allen
Daniela Gana
Dawn Morrison
Deb Evon
Donna Mann
Doogie Glassford
Dori-Ann Granger
Dragonwing
Elaine Milner
Elke Zimoch
Eric Bateman
Erin O'Kelly
Ernesto Montalve
Eugenia George
Eva Gorup
Ewelina Sparks
Faith Nelson
Francine Seal
Gemma B
Glenwood Bretz
Greg Miranda
Hanna Tetens
Heather Wittman
Heiko Ludwig

Holly Doyne
Hope Terrell
Irina Barnay
Isabella Leigh
Jane Lawson
Jean Schara
Jennette Marie Powell
Jennifer Sakaida
Jess
John Toppins
Joyce Sully
Juneta Key
Justin Colucci
Kara
Kari Wolfe
Karin Hernandez
Kathy Draxlbauer
Kim Lambert
Kirsten Bolda
Ken Bristow
Kristen Shields
Kyralae Bredi
Linda George
Liza Olmsted
Lizzie Merrill
Lynda Washington
madamebadger
Mary E. Merrell
Mary Wockenfuss
Marya Miller
Maureen Morley
Meagan Smith
Misti Pyles
Misty DiFrancesco

Moley
Nancy Nielsen-Brown
Nicola Lane
Panos
Pat Hauldren
Patricia Masserman
Paula C Meengs
Peggy Elam
Rebecca Wade
Rebecca Yeo
Reetta Raitanen
Ruth Sard
Sarah Brewer
Scorpion Gulch Studio
Simon Sawyers
Stacie Arellano
Susan Osthaus
Susan Witts
Sylvie Granville
Tammi Labrecque
Tammy L Breitweiser
Teresa Horne
Thomas Vetter
Tim King
Tiny Yellow Tree
Tuff Gartin
Vanessa Wells
Vorona
Wednesday McKenna
Zeyana Musthafa

About the Author

I'm a commercial novelist who went indie.

Lots of reasons, all good but none easy. In July of 2011 I walked away from commercial publishing to pursue *My Career My Way*, and it's been interesting times ever since.

Now I'm back to writing the *Cadence Drake*, *Moon & Sun*, and *Longview* series, creating stand-alone fiction, building writing courses, and getting the chance to speak directly to the readers of both my fiction and nonfiction.

If you keep hoping I'll do a particular story, or book, or course, and I haven't yet—let me know.

Cheerfully,
Holly Lisle

P.S. To find out what's coming next, and let me know what you'd love to see next…

Get my email updates:

https://hollyswritingclasses.com/go/pick-adventure-or-plain-emails.html

which come in two flavors…

- *Role-Playing-Adventure Game*

- *Plain emails*

When you sign up, the first thing you do is select the version of me you prefer.

After that, you either discover all the cool things I have to offer by playing through an email adventure…

Or by getting one email a week that takes you on a tour of my sites, books, classes, and other cool things.

(There are neither giant snakes nor mermaids in the "ordinary emails" version.)

Replies to emails come straight to me. Can't answer all of them, but I read them all, and answer when I can.

Find me here: HollyLisle.com

And here: HollysWritingClasses.com

Also by Holly Lisle

Cadence Drake & Settled Space Stories

Hunting the Corrigan's Blood — A Cadence Drake Novel

Warpaint — A Cadence Drake Novel

Born from Fire: Tales from The Longview — Episode 1

The Selling of Suzee Delight: Tales from The Longview —Episode 2

The Philosopher Gambit: Tales from The Longview —Episode 3

Gunslinger Moon: Tales from The Longview — Episode 4

Vipers' Nest: Tales from the Longview — Episode 5

The Owner's Tale: Tales from the Longview — Episode 6

The Longview Chronicles: The Complete Longview Collection

My Other Novels

The Ruby Key: Moon & Sun I

The Silver Door: Moon & Sun II

The Emerald Sun: Moon & Sun III (in progress now)

Talyn: A Novel of Korre

Hawkspar: A Novel of Korre

Midnight Rain (reprinted as By Kate Aeon)

Last Girl Dancing (reprinted as By Kate Aeon)

I See You (reprinted as By Kate Aeon)

Night Echoes (reprinted as By Kate Aeon)

My Fiction Singles

Strange Arrivals: Ten Tiny, Twisty Fantasy Tales

My Fiction in Collections

"Light Through Fog," The Mammoth Book of Paranormal Romance
"4EVR," The Mammoth Book of Ghost Romance
"Last Thorsday Night," The Mammoth Book of Time Travel
"Knight and the Enemy," The Enchanter Reborn
"Armor-ella," Chicks in Chainmail
"A Few Good Men," Women at War

My Nonfiction

Find these at HollysWritingClasses.com

FREE INTRO CLASS: How to Write Flash Fiction that Doesn't Suck
How to Write a Novel
How To Revise Your Novel
How To Write A Series
How To Think Sideways: Career Survival School for Writers
Create A Character Clinic
Create A Plot Clinic
How to Write Page-Turning Scenes
Create A Language Clinic
Create A Culture Clinic
Create A World Clinic
How to Write Short Stories
How to Write Villains

How to Find Your Writing Voice

How to Write Dialogue With Subtext

Title. Cover. Copy. Fiction Marketing

7-Day Crash Revision

21 Ways to Get Yourself Writing when Your Life Has Just Exploded

How to Find Your Writing Discipline

How To Motivate Yourself

How to Beat Writer's Block